D0644640

PETTICOATS *and Promises*

PENELOPE FRIDAY

Bella BOOKS
2015

Copyright © 2015 by Penelope Friday

Bella Books, Inc.
P.O. Box 10543
Tallahassee, FL 32302

All rights reserved. No part of this book may be reproduced or transmitted in any form or by any means, electronic or mechanical, including photocopying, without permission in writing from the publisher.

Printed in the United States of America on acid-free paper.

First Bella Books Edition 2015

Editor: Shelly Rafferty
Cover Designer: Linda Callaghan

ISBN: 978-1-59493-422-3

PUBLISHER'S NOTE

The scanning, uploading, and distribution of this book via the Internet or via any other means without the permission of the publisher is illegal and punishable by law. Please purchase only authorized electronic editions, and do not participate in or encourage electronic piracy of copyrighted materials. Your support of the author's rights is appreciated.

About the Author

Penelope Friday is a UK author who fell in love with the Regency in her teens, after becoming obsessed with Jane Austen's novels. As well as writing fiction set in the period, Pen also writes articles for *Jane Austen's Regency World*, which allows her to be excessively and gleefully geeky about the whole period.

When not writing, Penelope has an unusual range of interests including knitting, *Dr. Who*, children's literature and football (soccer).

Dedication

To James and Cameron
I am blessed

Acknowledgment

First, many thanks to JL Merrow and Shelly Rafferty, both of whom helped me edit Petticoats to within an inch of its life at various stages of its evolution. Thanks and/or apologies to the real Serena whose name I stole for my heroine—yes, she was named for you! And last but not least, love to my family and friends, who are the most supportive, wonderful people in the world.

1815

CHAPTER ONE

January

"Serena, darling!" My mother called as I walked past the open door of the parlour.

"Yes, Mama?"

Mama smiled up at me, her lap a mess of fashion plates sent down from London. "I'm thinking this one for morning wear," she said, pointing to an elegant, understated dress of plain muslin. "But do you think in pale green or in yellow?"

My coming out ball was a few scant weeks away, on the first day of March and my debut in London timed for shortly afterward. Clothes—accessories—ball preparation: these things were filling the minds of my mother and me.

Indeed, I believe my mother was almost as overexcited about the occasion as I was, and although my father pretended that he was just humouring the women in his life, I think he too felt a deep interest in his heart.

"Oh no," Mama corrected herself, not waiting for my answer. "Not yellow. If we could dress you in a bright buttercup yellow, perhaps, but with your beautiful dark hair"—she reached up and touched me lightly on the head—"pale yellow will look too dull, don't you think? Now Clara, I imagine, would look beautiful in pale primrose."

Clara was not, as you might think, my sister, but my closest friend. Our fathers had been fast friends since the days of their Grand Tour. As they lived less than five miles apart, in the two largest houses in Winterton, Clara and I were thrown regularly into each other's company. For the first eighteen years of our lives we played together: dressing dolls, fighting dragons, and sharing secrets. There was no one in the world, not even my own mother, who knew me as well as Clara did; certainly there was no one I loved better. I had no siblings—Clara, only one, a younger brother—but I felt no sense of something missing. Clara took the place of playmate, confidante, and sister, all in one."

"Mauve?" I suggested uncertainly. There were so many confusing rules about what a debutante might and might not wear, I found it hard to keep track. Certainly pastel shades were expected, but whether there were limits even within those, I was not sure. A pale purple *sounded* innocent enough, but who knew?

My mother looked me up and down, thoughtfully. "Mauve," she repeated. Then she smiled. "Yes, why not? Mauve it is. And now, what about hats and gloves?"

I sat down beside her, and we talked ball arrangements for the next hour, until we were called for lunch. But Mama was not the only person with whom I talked about the upcoming debut. Between Clara and me, it was also an oft-discussed subject.

Our fathers had agreed that we might share the occasion, which suited Clara and me. Doing anything, let alone participating in something so world-changing as this ball—*The Event* of our young lives—without my friend was unthinkable. Clara and I sat in her room one afternoon, talking, and our conversation turned to our futures.

"Of course," Clara said wisely, "one's debut is equivalent to announcing one's availability in the marriage market."

My own thoughts had been resting more on the idea of dancing and late nights. I gave Clara an anxious look.

"Do you think so?"

"Certainly." She nodded her head. "My mother has been giving me reams of practical advice as to how to ensnare a man." She mimicked Lady Maria's refined tones. "'Remember, my dear'" (Clara's mother always referred to her as "my dear," with limited truth), "'gentlemen do not like a lady to be too forward. Pray rein in your usual vigour; your manner should be more sedate. And make sure never to venture an opinion of your own.'"

I giggled. The idea of Clara lasting ten minutes without giving her opinion on each and every thing that caught her fancy was ridiculously improbable. Clara grinned at me.

"Now, now, Serena," she said with mock seriousness, "there is no need to take that attitude. Catching a husband is a solemn business, you know."

I fiddled with a strand of my hair, wrapping it round my finger.

"My mama only told me to be sure not to drink too much champagne," I confessed. "You don't…you don't really think that we are expected to marry in our first season, do you?"

"Why not? We don't want to run the risk of being left on the shelf," Clara retorted.

"I don't think I'd mind." I tugged at my hair nervously, and Clara slapped at my hand.

"You're too old to still be doing that, Serry." Then her tone changed. "Can't you imagine, though, how much nicer it would be to have a house of one's own? Not to have to listen to 'Clara, my dear, do this'; 'Clara, behave with a little more decorum' all day long?"

I said nothing for a second, trying to put my thought into words.

"But wouldn't you be swapping one duty for another?" I ventured. The words of the wedding ceremony flitted through my mind. "To love, honour, and obey…"

She shook her head. "Oh no, I'd only marry someone who would give me my own way in everything." She flashed a smile at me. "Someone like you."

"I don't want to marry." The words forced themselves out of me, unbidden.

Clara looked at me. I don't know what she saw in my face but her own expression softened. "Why not?"

"I wouldn't want to marry someone I didn't love," I said, "and…and…"

"And what, Serry?"

"I can't imagine loving anyone as much as I love you," I finished simply.

For a second Clara was silent. "You mean that?"

"Yes."

Her hand slipped into mine, her blue eyes gentle. For a long time we looked at each other, then Clara unexpectedly leaned toward me, an expression on her face I had never seen there before. "Serry," she said quietly, "I—"

There was a soft tap on the door. Clara jerked back, her sentence unfinished.

"Interrupting secrets?" teased my mother as she pushed the door open. However, she left no room for a reply, instead smiling across at me. "Come, Serena," she said. "It is time we were leaving for home—if, that is, I can drag your father away from his godson!"

We laughed. Clara's younger brother, Horace Battersley, was my father's namesake and godchild. Father maintained that by spending time with Horace-the-younger, he was merely doing his duty as a godfather—a fiction that I fear the rest of us didn't even pretend to believe was true. As we all knew, it was my father who had dragged his godson out to fly a kite that afternoon, not the other way around! Similarly, I could not conceal my unwillingness to leave Clara. I desperately wanted to know what she had been about to say, but since our childhood Mama had been used to tearing us apart despite cries of woe, and she saw nothing strange in my behaviour.

"Come now," Mama said, gently but firmly, and with a last wistful look at Clara, I stood.

* * *

I had too long to wonder what Clara might have said if Mama had not interrupted us. I saw the tableau in my mind: Clara, her blond hair escaping (as it so often did) from its restraints and fluttering down around the sides of her face. She had been leaning forward, her hand in mine, and those words on her lips. "*Serry…I—*" What had she been about to say? And, indeed, what had I wanted her to say? To tell the truth, I hardly knew; yet there was something—something. Oh, how I wished Mama had not chosen that particular moment to come in!

* * *

Two weeks later, a stroke of good fortune for my father meant that Clara and I would again have a chance to be alone. As Father looked up from his post at breakfast, he announced with pleasure that he had received excellent news.

"About what?" my mother asked.

"The East India Company." Father was beaming. "Profits have trebled since last year. I knew it! I knew that the future lay in trade between countries. Did I not say so?"

Mama smiled lovingly at him across the dishes. "You did indeed. I'm so glad, my dear."

"Now that that rascal Napoleon has been laid by his heels, the company will go from strength to strength," prophesied my father. "It was only that wretched war which brought so many problems. Well! I think this calls for a celebration, don't you agree?"

"Certainly," my mother agreed. "You mean to invite the Battersleys for dinner, I take it?"

"For dinner?" Father waved an indignant hand. "They must stay for the night, Elizabeth! You will arrange all that is necessary, I know."

"Of course I will," Mama said. "Perhaps," she added teasingly, "that is wiser than obliging them to drive home so late—or perhaps I should say, so early—after you and Mr. Battersley have been celebrating with a glass of champagne, and then a few more. I know how these evenings end up!"

"Now, Elizabeth!" my father protested. "Think of the impression you must be giving of me to your daughter!" But he was laughing, and we both joined in.

"All the same," said Mama to me after Father had left the table, "I don't imagine that Lady Maria will find the same satisfaction in the news as your father has. In her opinion, trade—whether successful or not—is beneath the notice of any true gentleman. Oh well. We must trust that she will say nothing to distress Father. And," she added, smiling at me, "I don't doubt you are filled with delight at the idea that Clara will stay. Perhaps it is just as well that Horace is back at school, though; it will be trouble enough with three guests. What Mrs. Brown will say, I do not know." By virtue of having held the role for more years than anyone cared to remember, our housekeeper was not backward about coming forward with her opinion on everything that happened in the household. It seemed all too likely that she would not appreciate being told she needed to make up three beds by the following evening. "Well, I shall not find out by sitting and waiting," Mama said as she stood, bustling away even before she had finished speaking.

I found that my heart was beating in a most peculiar way at the idea that I was to see Clara again. It seemed to speed, and then halt, until I felt almost sick. With the gentlemen celebrating in style, and Mama entertaining Lady Maria, it was certain that Clara and I would get some time alone. Would she tell me what it was that she had been about to say? Or would she have thought better of whatever impulsive utterance it might have been? At one moment I felt I could not wait until I saw her; at the next, I feared what she might say.

Two evenings later, I found the arrival of Clara and her parents strange, however—simply because everything appeared just as it ever did. The carriage pulled up a prompt five minutes before it was due—Lady Maria was a strong believer in punctuality, which in her mind equated to always being early—and the Battersleys descended. Mr. Battersley, as usual, was smiling jovially, already looking around for my father. Clara tumbled out of the barouche in slapdash fashion, more haste than elegance, and was rebuked by her mother for her lack of care. Finally, Lady Maria stepped down, her evening dress as neat and fashionable, but her expression one of barely concealed distaste. It was hard on the woman; Clara's father and mine had their shared youth and schooldays to bind them, and Clara and I were warm, devoted friends. Lady Maria and my mother, however, coped with each other's company in smiling mutual antipathy. Save having daughters of roughly similar ages, I dare swear they had not a single thing in common. My mother was interested in the neighbourhood, in all the minutiae of daily life in Winterton. She spent time with the villagers, knew all of them by name and a good deal about their situations, and took a genuine interest in their lives. She was always ready to help if asked, but never pushed her assistance on anyone who did not wish it. It was a delight to walk into the village with her and see people's faces light up simply because they saw her. Clara's mother, on the other hand, would (I often thought) have preferred it if no one breathed the same air as she, let alone lived close by. The idea of taking an interest in other people was frankly bewildering to her, and especially any interest in those of a lower social class than her own. She had her husband, her children and her dogs (the dogs probably the most loved of the three): who needed more? An evening in our company was more tribulation than joy to Lady Maria, as Mama and I knew all too well from previous experience. The Battersleys had visited many times in the past, and Mama had once commented that the only time she ever saw Lady Maria smile was when she left. This occasion, therefore, was no different to any other—on the surface. The difference lay only inside me, in the way I found myself staring at Clara as if we were meeting for the first time, in the curious sense of shyness which overcame me. But Clara soon swept away any reticence on my behalf as she bounced toward me, her eyes gleaming with pleasure.

"Hello, Serry! We've arrived!"

Behind her, I heard Lady Maria cluck disapprovingly at her exuberance, but as Clara took both my hands and swung me round in a circle, I found it hard to care. Then she was off, chattering about this and that which had happened since we'd last been able to talk, telling me how much she'd missed me.

"It has only been a couple of weeks," I protested.

"Has it?" Clara's voice changed; she sounded almost wistful. "It seems longer."

"Yes," I said quietly, "it does." I glanced up to where my father was in enthusiastic dialogue with Mr. Battersley, while my mother was politely conversing with Lady Maria about the flowers currently blooming in her respective garden. Our garden would soon be ablaze with daffodils, currently just budding, but ready to produce bright yellow trumpets to sway in the March breeze. I rather suspected that Clara's mother found their vibrant colour vulgar; she much preferred the elegant snowdrops that presently graced her own land.

"Later," Clara whispered, her gaze following mine.

After which, of course, the evening seemed to crawl past. We all sat around politely in the drawing room, split up into three distinct pairings but close enough that there could be no private conversation. Over dinner, chatter bounced among everyone at the table. Clara and I joined in the discussions with as much vigour as any of the adults. I was used to this; my parents had always encouraged me to speak when I chose, but I knew things were very different in Clara's house. Lady Maria firmly believed that children should be seen but not heard, but if indeed they must be heard, the best etiquette required one only to talk to the person on one's direct left or right side. General conversation was distinctly ill-mannered in her opinion. The subject of Napoleon's defeat and exile to Elba took centre stage, and was loudly acclaimed—not only on nationalistic grounds but because it had, after all, led to my father's trade success.

It was only later, when we were excused to retire to our rooms, that Clara and I got our first moments of privacy. I took Clara to her bedchamber (there was no real need, since she always had that room when she stayed), and as I hesitated between leaving and staying, Clara caught my hand.

"Serena," she said urgently. "Stay."

She pulled me to the bed and perched herself on the edge. I sat next to her, thinking how outraged Mrs. Brown would be if she saw us: our housekeeper regularly informed me that beds were invariably ruined by the disgraceful modern habit of sitting on them.

"I missed you," I said.

"Yes." Clara gave me an uncertain look. "Last time we were together…" she began.

"Yes?"

"Serry," Clara said. "Oh, Serry."

My hand was still in hers, and she pulled me forward and tentatively kissed me on the lips. I gasped and drew back, but my hand stayed steadily in hers. My lips prickled where hers had touched, and my heart beat so hard that the throbbing echoed in my ears.

"I've wanted to do that for years now," Clara said slowly, "but I didn't dare."

Her words shocked me, both that Clara could have thought of such a thing and that there was anything—*anything*—that Clara did not dare to do. Clara had always been the braver of the two of us—she had been first to gallop on her horse, and the one to dream up our childhood adventures, dragging me into them by the hand if I showed any disinclination. The only thing I ever knew Clara to fear was her mother. Out of Lady Maria's sight, she would take on any battle or task without a moment's hesitation. I stammered something unintelligible.

"Are you angry?" asked Clara. She sounded nervous.

Angry? How could I be angry with her? How could I be angry with the girl I loved above any other; how could I be angry when she made me feel so…

"We oughtn't," I said uncertainly.

I knew it was wrong. Aside from the dutiful kisses one bestowed on relatives, any sort of embrace was to be saved for marriage. We had been told so, over and again. The fact that we had been warned only from men meant nothing: love, physical love between two girls was so wrong, so unnatural as not even to be spoken aloud. We had broken a strict taboo. If anyone, ever, found out, we would be parted for life.

"No," Clara agreed, her voice low. "I'm sorry, Serena."

And then it was I who leaned toward her, my mouth that pressed against hers, my arms that were closing round my love, my Clara, my dearest, dearest friend.

"Serena!"

And the words tumbled from my lips. "Clara, darling, we mustn't—we shouldn't—I must—I love you so much."

Then Clara was kissing me back, both of us fumbling and unsure at this new encounter. I could feel a wetness on my cheek and I realised that Clara—brave Clara—was crying. I held her tight—tight—tight, squeezed her against me and fiercely resented the layers of clothes between us. I wanted to snuggle up in bed with her as we had done as children, but the feelings I had for her now shared little with the innocent companionable emotion of childhood. I wanted…I didn't know what it was I wanted but I knew with a fierce passion that Clara was the only person in the world who could give it to me. We clung and kissed and clung and touched and kissed again, so many pent-up emotions bursting free and sweeping us into a river of desire where right and wrong, duty and conformity, did not exist.

"Serry?" Clara's voice was husky. "Serry, dearest."

Her fingers fumbled with the fastenings of my dress, her eyes searching mine for permission as she slid the hooks apart. She had helped me undress many times before, but not like this—not like this. She pushed the sprigged muslin down past my shoulders, and I wriggled free of it, pushing it onto the floor with little care.

"You. You too," I pleaded.

"If someone should come…" Clara hesitated.

"I don't care," I said, almost weeping with need. "Say we were trying each other's dresses, say anything. Please, Clara."

She reached out to me, her hands stroking my face before sitting up to press her lips against mine again.

"Do it for me, Serry."

I began to unlatch the hooks and eyes, pressing kisses against her petticoat as I exposed more and more of it. Her dress was beautiful but Clara herself was so much more so. When at last the garment fell to the ground, I stepped back, drinking her in.

"You're so beautiful."

"I need you," she said, pulling me back toward the bed. "Please."

And that "please" was all I needed. With tentative hands, I stroked her arms; then, more daringly, her body.

"May I?"

I did not think I could bear it if Clara refused me, but she did not. Instead, she put her hand over mine, pressing it against her breast. I could feel the way her nipple peaked against the soft cloth of her shift and petticoat, and the very touch set up a throbbing between my legs which was both wonderful and not enough. My body felt as if it had taken on a new life, alive in a way I had never known existed. Clara pulled me close again, wrapping her legs around mine and kissing my neck over and over.

I do not know how much time we spent like this; it might have been minutes, hours. But eventually we drifted down from the storm our lovemaking had created, and slowly realised where we were—what it was that we had been doing.

We caught our breath on Clara's bed, heads side by side on the pillow. It had all been so sudden—so unexpected. I had never been so aware of the extent of my feelings for Clara before that night; she, more aware (as always) had yet never anticipated fulfilling her desire. For the longest time we lay next to each other, looking and marvelling at this new, wonderful thing.

Clara suddenly lifted herself to an elbow. "We must never do this again," she said, heartbreak in her voice.

"No."

"They would part us, shut us away. I believe my mother would imprison me in the house, never let me out again."

I thought of Lady Maria. Certainly I could not imagine her having even the smallest corner of sympathy for her daughter's illicit love. My own mother, I knew, would be devastated, however much she wished me to be happy. Happiness should not come in such a form, even with the most permissive of parents.

"We must pretend this never happened," I said.

I do not know how fervently I believed my own words, even at the time. I knew we ought to go back to our old, chaste friendship; but simultaneously I found it hard to accept a future where I would never again hold Clara in my arms.

"I love you," whispered Clara in my ear. "I always shall."

"I, too." For a second I clung to her and could not let go. "Oh Clara, I love you so much." Reluctantly, I got to my feet, picked up my discarded dress and smoothed down the creases before I slipped it over my head. If I did not leave now, I was not certain that I ever could. But I knew that someone—a maid, perhaps, or even worse, Lady Maria herself—would come to demand why we had not parted for sleep, and the fear of discovery gave me the impetus to move. I refastened a couple of the hooks, enough that I would look appropriately dressed to anyone I passed in the corridor. I pressed a kiss to Clara's hand. "I will see you in the morning."

"Yes." Clara was subdued, and almost—almost—I ran back to her, but with a last loving look, I walked to the door.

CHAPTER TWO

January-February

My night was a restless one. The next morning, when I caught Clara's eye at the breakfast table, I could see that she had passed the night no better than I. My mother caught us yawning, and fondly scolded us about the iniquity of staying up late to chatter. I tried not to imagine what she would say if she knew of our far worse sin.

Having once held Clara in my arms, I missed her with an aching passion. Our prospective ball—once the zenith of my anticipation—now loomed darkly on the horizon. No longer a joyous occasion of dancing and laughter, it now represented the first rupture between Clara and myself. Whilst we had previously been encouraged to devote our affections to our friendship, now we were expected to look elsewhere: to see, perhaps, in every eligible bachelor a future mate. I felt a wave of nausea pass over me at the prospect.

We, in turn, would be looked over like fillies at a horse sale. Did we have the right looks, the right pedigree, to make a suitable wife? Would we make good breeders? I had once had girlish dreams of being whisked away by a tall dominating gentleman, to be cared for and benevolently tyrannised over; now I could think of little worse.

Mama's fond intentions for my debut, however, were thrown into disarray by a letter which arrived that morning. She shared the content at the breakfast table. I had, it seemed, been accepted for Presentation at St James's Palace in London a scant week before our ball was to occur in Kent. Clara's parents, too, once they returned home, would find a royal missive bearing the same news. Of course, it was unthinkable that we should miss the opportunity of being presented at court—it was of central importance to one's social standing in the season ahead; however, I overheard my mother murmur that it would have been useful if Her Royal Highness had given just a *little* more warning. Although my mother had already begun to make arrangements for my presentation dress (a truly epic design with more petticoats than one might normally wear in a month)—and Clara informed me, with a roll of her eyes, that Lady Maria had been preparing for the auspicious occasion of meeting royalty for several months—the timing of the event was hardly propitious. We would be obliged to go to London for the presentation, and spend but a few days there before driving back to Winterton in time for the ball.

"The poor girls will be quite done up by the time it is finished," said my mother, and then took Clara and me to task for laughing at this idea. "You little know," Mama said severely, "how much the social scene takes out of one." She relaxed into a smile, and said ruefully, "Or, at any rate, it did me—but then I never was particularly delighted by the process."

We laughed a bit more, since Mama's dislike for London was well-known in our families: if she even had to pass through the city on her way elsewhere, one would see her face drop.

* * *

Over the next few weeks, the mad scramble involved in organising our presentations in London at the same time as we endeavoured to make the preparations for the ball in Kent was thoroughly enjoyed by Clara and me—though I admit that our parents felt somewhat differently about it! But whilst our elders undertook all the awkward details, Clara and I revelled in being the centre of attention. For Clara, especially, this was a novelty. I, being an only child, was used to my parents lavishing a certain amount of attention on me, but Clara, who usually took a rather poor second place to her younger brother Horace, the Battersleys' son and heir, was filled with pleasure at being for the moment the person around whom the family world revolved. Our parents, therefore, might be struggling with one hundred and one anxious dilemmas—whether to open the house in London; how many days in advance of the presentation we should drive up to town—but Clara and I simply delighted in the excitement of the hurly-burly.

A side effect of the craziness, however, was that Clara and I rarely had a moment together alone to speak about the night on which our relationship had escaped from its years' old form and threatened to engulf us in its passion. Whenever I thought I might have a chance of seeing her, it was certain that my mother would call me to speak about dress fittings or one of the other multitudes of minor details relevant to my debut. Even our usual morning horse rides—arranged to occur simultaneously, with our fathers' encouragement—took second place to presentation arrangements. The presence of the grooms would, of course, have made private conversation difficult, but Clara had long ago worked out a way of "losing" our servants when she wished. They had scolded at first, but now were more resigned to "the little misses' ways." However, it seemed if I rode, Clara was kept at home by her mother and if she rode, I was.

"You'd think that they were positively trying to keep us apart," I said in frustration, after Clara and I met unexpectedly in the haberdashery in Winterton. I had been sent to buy green ribbon in a quantity which seemed quite out of proportion to my size; Clara, whose mother usually refused to frequent the local shops in favour of ordering from London, had an urgent need for buttons. Lady Maria was picking up one type and then another, anxiously attended by the shopkeeper, Miss Williams, as Clara and I huddled at the door and talked almost in whispers.

"Believe me," said Clara ruefully, checking to see that Lady Maria was not in hearing, "if my mother was able to keep us apart, she would. I believe she fears that I may take up some of your mother's 'frankly bourgeois' notions—the words are hers, not mine, I might add! Thank heavens for Papa, who doesn't give a rush about such things."

"It's fortunate that she doesn't know where Mama is now," I said, half-offended on my mother's behalf, who was visiting our groom's elderly parents whilst I dealt with the issue of the ribbon. "I imagine she would think that Mama's visit to Mr. and Mrs. Simons is bourgeois. Perhaps Lady Maria would rather that we let the families of our servants suffer in poverty?"

"Undoubtedly, if it meant that one didn't have to go near them," Clara agreed amiably. "And don't blame me. It's hardly my fault that my mother has some strange beliefs."

"Of course not."

I relaxed and smiled, and reached out to hold her hand. As our fingers touched I think we were both jolted by what felt like lightning quivering between us. As our eyes locked on one another, I was reminded irresistibly of our kiss, and we were almost overwhelmed by the desire to repeat it.

"Me too," whispered Clara, knowing what was in my mind. "Serry, me too."

Lady Maria finished her business with Miss Williams, and commandingly called Clara back to her side. We let go our grip. As they left the shop, I followed them out, and reluctantly watched until Clara was nearly out of sight. My mother's voice startled me back to the present.

"Do you have the ribbon?"

"Yes, Mama." I had lingered in the shop only to talk with Clara.

"Well done." She smiled at me. "And my business ended satisfactorily too. Simons won't need to worry about his parents now. I have told them to order what they need from the shops and send the bill to your father." She smiled. "Despite Lady Maria's oft-repeated opinion, I know that they will not take advantage of our good nature. On the contrary, they were embarrassed by the very offer. But I told them that if they did not order the food themselves, I would do it for them, and I think that will keep them in check. They would be mortified to put me to any further trouble, and they know I will stand by my word."

"I do love you, Mama," I said, grateful that Clara's mother was not my own.

My mother laughed, touched as well as disconcerted by the declaration. "Well, Serena darling, I'm glad to hear it." She tucked my arm more firmly through her own as we walked briskly back to our house.

* * *

Almost before I knew it, the days of arrangements were over and we were on our way to London, bearing what seemed to be enough clothes to last until May! I was thrilled, if a little bit anxious, to visit London. I had only been once in my life, when I was a small girl. My mother had taken me there to visit my Aunt Hester (known to the polite world as the Dowager Lady Carlton), and on this occasion we were to stay with my aunt again. My parents had decided not to open their town house, since the duration of our visit was so brief. In contrast, the Battersleys had opened their residence. I believe that Lady Maria would have considered it most demeaning either to beg accommodation of another person or to stay in an hotel. For myself, I was glad to be with my aunt, and to be part of a bustling, cheerful household. My cousin Anna, who was on the point, Mama told me, of forming a most appropriate betrothal, was at home. Three years older than I, she seemed to me the fount of all social knowledge, and to her credit she never got bored of my questions—or at any rate she never showed it.

Frederick, the present Lord Carlton, did not live with his mother, but he was invited to dinner in order to spend time with his family, and he had the good nature to wish me (albeit with a somewhat patronising air) the best of luck in my presentation. I was not altogether sure what would constitute luck on such an occasion, further than managing my train without tripping and prostrating myself full length at the Queen's feet; however, I took the comment in the spirit it was meant and thanked him kindly. Aunt Hester was due to present me, since court etiquette demanded that debutantes be presented by a titled lady. Lady Maria, of course, would be presenting Clara. My third cousin, Edward, was not at home. He was currently up at Oxford, where he was expected to do extremely well; his college had predicted great things for him, it seemed. I have to admit that given what I was told of his learning and knowledge, I could only be grateful that I did not have to face such a paragon of wisdom, for I felt sure he would despise me for all the things I did not know.

But no one could be frightened of Aunt Hester. She was, it seemed, a well-respected member of the *ton*; however, Anna told me that some of the highest sticklers disapproved of her mother because she was considered "too good-natured."

"She has even been known," Anna said, her eyes dancing, "to smile at young ladies with nothing in the way of fortune or family to recommend them—and that, you know, is at least a venial sin!"

"Everyone sounds terrifying," I said, having visions of quantities of Lady Marias thronging London balls and receptions.

Anna laughed. "Never fear, my dear. Despite her reputation, my mother is quite capable of administering a cutting set-down to those who criticise her, and she is very much looking forward to when you come down in a few weeks to start your season proper, when she hopes she will be able to chaperone us both around town, if your mother does not object too much."

"I'm sure my mother will be delighted," I said, able to imagine the look of relief on my mama's face when she heard Aunt Hester's plan.

"Mama doesn't want to usurp Aunt Elizabeth," Anna said, anxious not to be misunderstood.

"My mama is quite desperate to be usurped," I said, smiling, and told her of my mother's unconcealed loathing of town events.

Anna laughed. "Then this season will make two people happy—as happy, I hope, as you and I! You will enjoy London,

Serena, I guarantee it. Nobody—well, your mother excepted!—could fail to take pleasure in it. And I am looking forward to introducing my cousin to all my friends."

Anna was as genuine in her vicarious excitement for me as her mother was, and although I knew I would have Clara for support, it was pleasant to feel I would be surrounded by family and friends anxious to welcome me to London. I couldn't help showing off a little bit to Clara when we met the next morning in the park. Aunt Hester had assured me that it was "quite the thing" for a morning excursion, and it seemed Lady Maria felt the same way. But I'm afraid that London had rather gone to my head; rather than commenting on the joy of seeing Clara, the first words out of my mouth were:

"I'm so lucky to have my aunt to bring me out. She knows everything!"

Of course, Clara was not going to put up with that sort of remark. "My mother does too," she retorted, looking over to where Lady Maria was chatting decorously with my mother and aunt.

"But Aunt Hester is one of the most respected ladies in society," I persevered, determined to make my point.

"So my mother would be if we lived here. I'm sure she *will* be, once we take up residence in our London house for the season."

"Aunt Hester is on visiting terms with all the ladies who run Almack's."

"Well, Mother's on first-name terms with the Queen herself," Clara said in turn.

We looked at each other and burst out laughing at the ridiculous boasts to which we had pushed each other. Clara usually took the lead in any social occasion, since she always seemed to know the right things to say and was so very much more outgoing than I. But although I was usually happy to follow in her shadow, I couldn't help feeling that it would be rather agreeable to bask equally in the limelight when it came to our season. Aunt Hester, I knew, would be a valuable ally.

The presentation itself, I regret to say, was rather anticlimactic. After several hours with my mother and my maid,

Alice, I was finally dressed. My hooped skirt stuck out in such a way as to make it almost impossible to sit down, used as I was to simpler high-waisted dresses. My hair was weaved through with white feathers—utterly out of fashion in every other situation, but the court still required a certain number of these in a debutante's dress. I was prodded and prinked and fussed over until I felt exhausted, and longed for home. I hoped and trusted that the events of the season would not all follow this pattern, and my mother assured me that it would not.

Uncomfortable but resplendent in my finery, I kissed the elderly Queen's hand before backing away to return to my place in the line of other debutantes. Clara had been the first to approach Queen Charlotte (my dreams of metaphorically leading the way would have to wait for the season itself) and she performed the curtsey and obeisance with an air of elegance that neither I nor any other girl could match. I did not fall over my feet, though I saw another girl stumble, and watched her face crimson with mortification. I would have smiled at her, but I feared she might see it as gloating at her distress rather than the sympathy I intended. It was too hot, too crowded, and too dull for me to feel anything except relief when the drawing room ceremony ended.

The evening was more interesting, however. Aunt Hester pointed out various leaders of society, and I even exchanged a few words with His Royal Highness, the Duke of Clarence, something I confess that I found more pleasure in looking back upon than in the experience itself, where I was tongue-tied with nervousness. But the Duke must have been used to bashful debutantes; he answered at least one of his own questions, and smiled at me with great affability before moving on to thrill another girl.

At least Clara and I managed to spend some time together that evening, though we had little time to exchange anything but small pleasantries.

"My mother," Clara informed me solemnly when we found ourselves together at the edge of the room, "is somewhat taken aback by the standing your aunt has in society. She knew that

Lady Carlton was well-thought of, of course, but it seems she had not realised that she was also your aunt."

I had pointed out Clara to my aunt, and she had commented favourably on Clara's looks and bearing. "Aunt Hester thinks you look beautiful," I told her, my eyes telling her that I too felt this. I wondered how I could never before have realised what we shared; wondered too how no one else seemed to have discovered it. My love for Clara was so strong that even in a situation such as our presentation it overwhelmed any other emotion.

"Serry," she said quietly, her breath catching a little and her hand flying to touch mine, just for a second. Recovering herself, she said lightly, "Well, Mother said that she 'never would have thought' that you could look so elegant."

We both giggled at the remark, from Lady Maria, it was intended as a great compliment, but I fear we were unimpressed.

Nevertheless, after the stress of the presentation itself, I was inclined to think the evening a complete success, and found myself looking forward to my season once more, despite the division I still feared might grow up between Clara and myself. It was almost a disappointment to wake up the next morning to find my parents ready to return to Kent. I would, had I been asked at that moment, have given up the home ball in preference to staying with Aunt Hester. But I was not asked, and I did not say, and I knew that without Clara in town my pleasure would not be half so great. Instead, therefore, we set out for Winterton in good time, and I spent several happy hours in the carriage remembering the high points of my soon-to-be-repeated time in town.

CHAPTER THREE

February-March

The last few days back in Kent leading up to our local debuts passed quickly. The trip to London had inevitably diverted us away from our own preparations at home; now, with barely two days to go before the ball would take place, we discovered a multitude of finer points which required our immediate attention.

Minds were distracted for a short while when we heard rumours that the bogeyman Napoleon had escaped from Elba, but for Clara and me this news held little interest compared to the drama of our own coming out. I am ashamed to recall how insular we were, how little involved in one of the most major events of our time. Our parents, of course—my father, particularly—listened for each new bit of information avidly, but even their involvement became buried beneath a sea of the important nothings which accompanied the arranging of a ball.

"It's concerning," Father said, frowning a little as he turned the pages of his newspaper. "Boney was supposed to be safe, and now…"

I sighed inwardly. Who could possibly care about a villain far abroad when there was a ball to be arranged? Yet Father seemed to speak of nothing else. Thankfully, Mama interrupted him with a subject far more to my taste.

"Horace," she said, interrupting his perusal of the news, "Lady Ratchett has just sent a note to inform us that her son *will* be attending the party after all. Please instruct the men to allow him access; she says he may be a little late."

My father responded appropriately, but two minutes later, I saw that he was buried back in his paper again. My mother and I exchanged glances and sighed.

Clara and I were required to play our part in proceedings far too often to allow us a great deal of time alone, and in any case, a strange sort of shyness had overtaken us. We had quick, superficial conversations in which we spoke of everything save that which affected us most. I knew that we must never touch each other again, just as we had agreed—yet, when I was alone, I found myself reliving those instants we'd had together. Sometimes I felt guilty; more often, however, I simply felt a deep sense of longing. Clara and I belonged together—we always had. Knowing that we could never be together, that our love was forbidden, made this thought no less compelling. By the evening of the ball itself, however, I had gone over our moments of desire so many times in my head that they seemed more a dream than reality.

Still, there was no denying that part of my pleasure in the idea of the ball had seeped away. My mother could not help but notice. Putting it down to nerves, she set herself to reassure me as she instructed and assisted the maid to dress me.

"There is nothing to fear, Serena," she told me as Alice brushed carefully and thoroughly at my thick, straight hair. "I know you and Clara have been looking on this evening as an occasion; and that is quite natural and understandable—but it is meant for you to enjoy. I remember at my first dance..." and she rambled on comfortably, her reminiscences interspersed with instructions to Alice to be sure and smooth my dress neatly; to remove the dirt mark her motherly eyes had spotted on my glove; to move the necklace just a little, so it hung down evenly.

Clara, I knew, was being overseen by her own mother—albeit with less comfort and more instruction on etiquette coming her way. We had discussed our dresses in detail with each other, but had agreed that they should stay unseen until the ball itself. I knew that Lady Maria had insisted on the starkest of whites, which she claimed would look perfect with Clara's delicate pink-and-white colouring. But when I caught my first glimpse of my friend, I could only stand and stare.

Lady Maria had been correct. In her debutante ball gown, Clara was stunningly beautiful. She wore a coronet in her hair topped with a single pearl, and the corsage of flowers she wore—purple irises—gave the only spot of colour to her dress. Beside her, in my cream gown (the pink rosebuds insipid next to Clara's dashing irises), I felt dowdy and uncomfortable. But the look Clara gave me restored my confidence. There was something in her eyes that reminded me of the moment before she'd kissed me, and I longed for her to do so once more. Instead, though, we caught each other's hands and admired one another in silence.

It was a frightening time for me, or would have been without Clara's support. We stood by the doorway, welcoming the guests—speaking to stranger after stranger after barely known acquaintance. Clara had the poise that I lacked, and she laughed and chattered as I fought for the words that tripped so easily off her tongue. But Clara drew me into the brief conversations, and encouraged me to show myself to my best advantage. I might not want to marry any of the guests, but at the same time I did not want to be shown up as a country bumpkin. Perhaps I might be vain, but I wanted them at least to consider the prospect of marrying *me*, even if I had no interest in them!

Our cards were marked with our partners, and the ball began. As it was taking place at Clara's house, it was she who led the couples out. I was content to take a secondary role, however, content to watch my love dance the figures and to follow where she led. I had never seen a gathering of so many people, and I was stunned by the heat and the noise, but at the same time I loved every second—the dancing, the drinks, the beautiful attire of the ladies and gentlemen. After a glass of champagne, I began to relax and enjoy myself, and I could see Clara doing the same.

My happy mood was not to last. Halfway through the ball, as I finished dancing with Edward Latimer, a man I had known since childhood, I looked up and caught a troubled expression on Mama's face.

"Excuse me," I said apologetically, as he offered to fetch me a drink, "but I must go to my mother." I knew better than to dash across the ballroom: I had no wish to draw attention to my mother's distress. Instead, I walked toward her as casually as I could. The mask slipped only when I was by her side. "Mama, what's wrong?"

My mother forced a smile.

"Nothing, dear, why do you ask?"

I had never known her to lie to me, and my suspicion of some intentional deceit was in itself more frightening than any truth might have been.

"What has happened?" I demanded urgently. I grasped her hand and held it between my own.

Her eyes fixed steadily on my own, her voice but a whisper. "I need you to be brave, Serena," she said quietly. "I need you to return to the ball as if nothing has happened. Can you do that one thing for me?"

I nodded and squeezed her hand. If my silence was all I could do for her, I would keep my counsel. I paused a second, as the careless, laughing crowd turned about the room, and wondered whether any of them knew my mother's secret. Clara danced past with her partner—a soldier who had received a major injury eighteen months earlier in the Battle of Leipzig. One of his legs was undeniably shorter than the other, but as he danced, his face showed no trace of the anxiety I saw in my mother's. Whatever had upset her appeared to be only a family matter.

I looked around for my partner for the next dance, a Mr. Feverley. He was a timid, young red-headed gentleman who stammered his request and looked appalled rather than grateful for my acceptance. He came hesitantly to meet me, still apparently deciding whether to dance or run, but his ambivalence was just what I needed. I began to forget my own troubles (and I still did not know what they were) even as I allayed his. I smiled at him encouragingly, and he managed the final few steps to my side with only the smallest of stumbles.

"Thank you for asking me," I said, as he tripped toward me.

"My...my mother—I mean...my pleasure..."

My smile broadened. I recognised his mother from the hunted glance over his shoulder: a formidable woman who was determined that all of her relations should marry above their station.

"Don't worry," I murmured as the music started up again. "It's only a dance, not a proposal to wed."

Red-haired as he was, his face mirrored his scalp.

"It's not—I don't mean..."

"I know," I soothed, and grasped his hand a little tighter. "Just relax and enjoy it. If truth be known, I'm as shy as you are. So let's forget about it and dance."

If only it were that easy. Throughout the rest of the evening, despite the distraction of the dance, my eyes kept searching out my mother. She seemed relaxed enough on the surface, but I could see her whole body droop when she thought that no one was looking. My father, too, looked sterner than ever. He was not, in fact, a stern man, but his face in repose looked grim, and the result of anxiety was to strengthen the lines of his visage.

Mr. Feverley, however, seemed buoyed by my encouragement, and, it turned out, he was a very reasonable dancer when nerves had not the better of him. Similarly, his conversation was wittier than one would expect, to the point that I positively enjoyed his company. When we parted, he stammered out probably the most honest compliment I ever heard.

"Th-thank you, Miss Coleridge. I have never enjoyed a dance before."

I smiled at him, and felt a strange sense of motherliness toward him. "You're a good dancer, and I enjoyed myself greatly. Thank you."

He mumbled something, as an attack of bashfulness overtook him, and edged off sheepishly to find his mother.

The rest of the ball passed in something of a blur. I am not sure whether it was the champagne (for that first glass had not been my only one), my worry for my parents, or the noisy late night, but it seemed that one moment it was eleven o'clock, and the next it was three in the morning, the carriages bumping off down the drive full of exhausted, happy ladies and gentlemen. Clara still sparkled with excitement, but even she was subdued, tired out by a night of constant music, dancing, and attention. We were staying at the Battersleys' house overnight; my mother had been convinced that I would be too worn out by the exigencies of the ball even for the short trip back to our house, and Mr. Battersley had taken little persuasion to agree to host his best friend's family for a little longer.

"To bed," Lady Maria said, with the authority of someone used to unconditional obedience.

I met my mother's eyes for a second, but she gave a slight shake of her head. Now was not the time, it seemed, for disclosure of whatever secret was worrying her. I nodded my acquiescence and followed Clara up the stairs, where we had time only for the briefest of remarks before Lady Maria chased us apart.

* * *

I slept heavily, thanks to the mixed effects of exhaustion and alcohol, but as soon as I woke the following morning, my mind was filled not with memories of the dancing and music, but of the image of my mother's worried face. I still had no idea what it was that had upset her, and I could bear to wait no longer. Before I had even dressed, I dashed along the corridor to her room and rapped on the door.

"Mama! Mama?"

My mother, wrapped in her negligee, opened the door.

"Serena, dear," she said softly. "Come in. There is no need to wake the house."

Mama closed the door behind me.

"Now," I said, as I lowered myself onto the edge of her bed, "tell me."

Mama's lips were pressed together, and I could see a crease between her eyes. Although she had allowed me in, she seemed disinclined to talk, and I knew something was very wrong indeed. But the silence after my demand weighed her down.

"I am sorry," she began, "so terribly sorry…"

"What is it?" I demanded again, made more anxious by her difficulty in getting to the point.

"Your father has lost a great deal of money," she said bluntly.

"How?" I stood up in my dismay. "Last night?"

"Last night we received confirmation," Mama told me. "We had been hoping…but it was not to be."

"Mama, please tell me," I begged. "What has happened?"

"Napoleon," Mama said. "Napoleon has happened."

"But…" It was several days since the first rumours of Napoleon's escape had proven true; Napoleon had ceased to be current gossip, and we had fallen back into our old ways once more. "We knew that already. And how can Father's—how can this be related to Napoleon?"

"The bulk of Father's money relies on his being a stockholder with the East India Company," my mother began. I had known this, of course, but I could not see the link between the company and Napoleon. East India was not, after all, France. "Trading has not ceased, and we hoped that we could make our way through this difficult time. But the stocks have plummeted now that we are no longer in utter control of the seas." She paused. "Stock-market trading has been frozen in certain areas; Father can neither sell nor gain interest from his shares. In short, all the money bound up in the company is gone."

"Gone? How much?" I had visions of our house being taken from us, our family turned onto the streets, all the servants given notice. I remembered my beautiful, expensive dress from the night before, and started calculating for how much it might be sold.

"You were a brave girl last night, Serena, and I need you to be brave again. There is no money for a season."

At first, I was overcome with relief. After the catastrophic imaginings I'd had, the news that I would not be going to London seemed to pale in comparison.

"Is that all?" The words had tumbled out of my mouth before I had time to think.

She nodded. "That's all." She hesitated a second. "But darling, I'm not sure you realise what a difference it will make.

I know you enjoyed the ball last night, despite everything—but it was the first and last time."

"You mean…"

"From now on, Serena, you will have to stay home. You will watch Clara do on her own all the things you had planned to do together, and you must be brave about it."

The thought hadn't even come to me before then. "Clara—Clara still goes to London?"

"Yes."

I rushed to the window, and looked out in a vain hope to hide my woe from Mama. Clara would go, and I would stay. We would be parted—parted for months. I had seen her near every week of my life, and for her to go now, just when we had discovered that we had something special…I found the tears rolling down my face.

"Serena," my mother said quietly, "I know it is hard. But please remember that it is a difficult time for us all, especially for your father. If he could change things so that you were not affected, he would."

"I know." I couldn't stop my voice from quavering, though I tried. "I know. I—"

I broke off and ran from the room, back to my own chamber, where I could weep in private. It was not that Mama was unsympathetic, nor that I did not know that things might have been considerably worse. But—oh! My dreams of dancing and friendship and Clara, Clara, *Clara*! We would have been together most days, making visits or attending dances or breakfasts. I had not realised how much I had relied on the simple fact that I would be with her. It was not the season itself that I felt so bitterly upset about, but the fact that Clara and I would be separated. Was this perhaps my punishment for what I had done? For committing the sin of kissing Clara, I would now be separated from her forever. Or so it felt, to my young mind.

Alice entered the room when I had passed the peak of my sobbing fit and was beginning to quieten down into the hiccupping stage. She had been my maid for many years, and she knew better than to comment on my sadness. Instead, she silently produced my clothes for the day and began to help me into them. In her wordlessness I found a strange comfort: I knew that she was expressing sympathy as she arranged my undergarments and then my dress with gentle hands. I wiped away the last of the tears and gave her a watery smile.

"No London for us, Alice—you heard?"

"Yes, miss. A shame, but not a tragedy." Alice was always full of homespun wisdom.

I sniffed, but nodded. "You're quite right."

"Anyhow, you look fit to be seen, miss," Alice said as she added the last touches to my hair.

"Thank you."

I took a final look in the mirror to check that my face had not become too blotchy. It was one thing to cry, another to be seen looking a state in public. Apart from my own pride, I had my father's status to uphold. However upset I might be, I would not let him down by showing my distress to all and sundry, especially not to Clara's parents. I would give Lady Maria no opportunity to look down on our family any more than she already did. It was with head held high that I went downstairs to partake of a late breakfast.

Clara was already seated at the table when I arrived, and despite my attempt to look unconcerned, she knew immediately that something was wrong. However, the presence of the servants and her mother gave her pause and, to my relief, Clara was for once discreet. When the meal was over, however, she dragged me off to my room and demanded to know what the matter was.

There was no point in hiding it. We had been due to travel to London in only two days' time, and my absence for the season would tell its own woeful story. But even if my mother had asked me to keep it secret, I could not have refrained from telling Clara. When I finished speaking, she leaned forward and grabbed my arms.

"You won't be in London?"

Miserably, I shook my head. "No."

Her fingers tightened around my wrists. "You must be," she insisted. "How can I manage without my Serry by my side?

We do *everything* together! You can't leave me to face it alone. Especially not now." I bit my lip between my teeth to try and stop myself from crying again. Clara saw the sadness in my face and softened immediately, and pulled me forward into her arms. "Serry, Serry, I'm sorry. It's worse for you, of course it is. It's just…" She kissed my neck, over and over. "…I'll miss you so much."

"We said we wouldn't…" I started weakly, but Clara interrupted me.

"I lied," she said. She pulled me even closer so that I half-lay across her lap. "We didn't know then that we would be parted so soon." She turned my face toward hers and pressed a kiss onto my lips. "I thought I would have time to persuade you round."

Her arms were around me, and she stroked my back with one gentle hand. With the other she wiped the few shed tears from my face, and then kissed the places where they had lain.

"Clara…" I whispered, but she put a finger across my lips.

"Shhh. This isn't the moment to speak. Just feel, darling."

She trailed kisses along my neck, and her hand stroked my hair, ruffling it from Alice's neat coiffure. I felt my body respond, and arched into her embrace so that we were breast to breast. My arm slid around her as easily and naturally as if we had done this all our lives; as if it was what we had been created to do. And when our lips met, it felt like a taste of heaven itself. Clara, my Clara, my love. For some moments—I do not know how long, it might have been a second or an eternity—we were lost in each other. I knew only that I wished it to last forever.

Then my mother called my name from the hallway, and life spun once more and settled in the new-old pattern. For soon, too soon, we would be parted.

CHAPTER FOUR

March-April

There were three days before Clara was to go to London, and the time seemed to speed away as they brought our separation nearer. Clara and I had one last moment alone together: when my parents and I returned to our own house later that day, Clara gained permission from her father to come with us. The carriage would pick her up in the evening, but for one glorious hour, Clara and I were alone in my bedchamber. With my parents discussing financial affairs, we were safe from interruption. Nevertheless, I dragged a chair against the door. It would give no more than a few seconds' warning, but it somehow lent an air of privacy to our togetherness. Clara and I sat on the bed itself, where we had shared so many secrets. This secret was the most private of all.

"Serry," Clara murmured, taking my hand and pressing an almost shy kiss to it.

"Yes."

My fingers closed on hers and—I do not know who started it but suddenly we were breast to breast, lips to lips, kissing as if we depended on each other for our very survival. Can I call it a kiss? It was so much more than just a meeting of lips. It was a meeting of desires, which flamed up between us until I felt as if my body was on fire. My fingers tugged at Clara's clothes, and this time I could not be satisfied just by removing the top layer of her dress. She felt the same way, each of us whimpered in frustration at the trials of her layers of petticoat and corset. Finally, we managed together to divest her of her clothes until she stood just in her shift. And oh, she was beautiful. So beautiful. There was a look of hesitancy in her face, as if she was not sure what I thought of her. But how could there be a doubt? The exquisite curves of her shoulder, the plumpness of her breasts; her skin a perfect cream-colour I longed to cover with kisses. I could have knelt at her feet and worshipped.

"You too," she said.

"I'm not beautiful like you." I was suddenly reluctant, fearful that my thin frame might not be appealing to her.

"So much more so," she said quietly, as her arms reached around me to unfasten my dress before pushing it to the floor. She had a look in her eyes which told me that yes, to her I truly was beautiful, despite my imperfections. How could I possibly believe myself unattractive whilst Clara's eyes looked at me with *such* adoration in them? "Your petticoat?" she pleaded.

I shrugged it over my head, and loosened the bindings of my corset until it all but fell away. Clara's fingers helped it down, lingering for a second on the side of my breast so that I took a sudden deep breath.

Then, both of us, semidressed, laid across the bed. Clara's hand was still on my breast, and as I lay close to her, I could feel the heat of her body, the quickened beating of her heart. I yearned for more, for her to touch me more—for her to allow me access to the secrets of her flesh. I moved my hand unsteadily across the thin chemise which covered her rounded belly, and she shivered and giggled at the sensation. I went to draw away, but she laid her hand on top of mine.

"No. Serry, darling—don't stop."

I kissed her mouth, her cheek, her neck; the more I was given, the more I desired. "Clara—my Clara."

She wrapped her legs around mine, pulled me close so that our bodies aligned from breast to ankle. "How am I going to bear London without you?" she murmured.

"Or how I, home?" I nuzzled her neck. "How can I lie in this bed, night after night, alone—after this?"

"I won't go without you—I won't!" Clara sounded angry, desperate. We both knew that she had no more choice than I; I must stay, and she must go.

"Shh..." And it was I who comforted her. I ran my fingertips in gentle circles over her back as I spoke. "It is not forever, my love. It is March, and Lady Maria will scarcely be so gothic as to remain in London in the summer. By early August, if not before, you will be home. It is not so long."

But my voice betrayed me: despite my good intentions, it wobbled at the thought of our parting. Five months was not, it was true, an eternity, but the days stretched long in front of me. Clara would have the thrill of London ahead; I only the same village as ever, missing Clara, who had always been the best part of my life there, even before our friendship had taken this deeper turn. Clara buried her head in my shoulder for a second. I could hear her hitched breathing as she fought against tears. I knew the moment she won the battle.

"Kiss me, Serry," she whispered, turning her face up to mine. "Make us forget what lies ahead."

* * *

Two days later, on a bleak morning in early March, Lady Maria drove over with Clara to say their farewells. The rain dashed against the windows, and the world outside appeared grey and dismal. Clara and I had not a moment to ourselves. Lady Maria made it all too clear that this was a courtesy call only, and that she was anxious to get away. If she had not enjoyed the company of my family when we were as well-off as she, she certainly didn't want to spend time with us now that our fortunes had fallen. It was evident that it was only thanks to the insistence of Clara's father that she had come at all. The visit was brief and as cold as the weather; when they left, it was I, sitting inside by a hot fire, who felt frozen through.

Time passed slowly, and soon I knew that the season had begun for Clara. It seemed almost deathly quiet without her; London was so far away. Not the faintest possibility existed that I might look up from my reading, as I had done so many times in the past, to see her trotting down the drive on Mimosa, her beloved grey horse. Worst of all was the knowledge that I must not betray how much I missed her, and in what ways; how much I longed for the touch of her fingers on my face, the whisper of her lips against my skin. I could imagine Clara dancing at balls, laughing and chatting with the other debutantes—of which I should have been one—drinking champagne and not retiring to bed until the early hours of the morning. I didn't begrudge Clara any of these things, but oh! How I wished I could be there too. I found my only consolation in her letters: fragments, usually, joined together in Clara's hectic style gave a stop-start idea of London gaiety. But always, she added wistfully, that she wished I were there. She chose these words more carefully than the rest so that should our parents catch sight of the note, they would see nothing amiss. But I could see, almost feel the depth of her longing for me, even in the midst of her season. And how much more so did I miss her!

Indeed, I was left so alone that I even had time to miss my governess, Miss Bruce, and attempted to learn a little history on my own account. But if learning had not always kept my attention even with an entertaining governess (for Miss Bruce had known how to share her knowledge with a pupil without boring her unnecessarily), it was almost impossible to concentrate amid my misery and loneliness. I would take up a book, intending to study it in depth, but before I had looked at more than the first few pages my mind would drift off into dreams of Clara, and I would come to some little time later, realising that I had taken in not a single word. The only time I found any level of contentment was when I wrote to my love. I poured out my heart in those letters, unable to keep to the pattern of the wisely-worded phrases Clara used. It was too difficult, when

I missed her lips against mine, her hand on my skin. I wrote the more mundane letters too—those for public consumption, which spoke about day-to-day life in Winterton—then enclosed my private missives inside them, always ending with the words "Burn this."

My mother bore with me well for a time; she understood that I needed a while to adjust. She gave me a little space to mope, but also asked regularly for my assistance in household tasks which I knew perfectly well she could have completed on her own. I had always wondered what went on in the private conversations between Mama and Mrs. Brown each morning; now I knew, and I found it difficult to care in the slightest. As the weather grew warmer, Mama encouraged me to go out and about, to ride with one of the grooms around the estate. But even riding Misty wasn't the same when Clara wasn't there with Mimosa, challenging me to races and giggling at the scandalised looks our galloping received from both our grooms and the local inhabitants, who clearly thought that no ladies would urge their horses faster and faster.

"Really, Clara," I would tease in my best Lady Maria fashion, "this *ventre a terre* riding is inappropriate in one so young and delicate."

"It is Serena, Mother," she would reply in turn. "She is such a bad influence on me—I scarcely know what I am doing when I am with her."

Sedate rides with a groom as my only company, therefore, did nothing to lift my mood, and eventually even Mama lost patience with me.

One morning, Mama's tolerance for my ennui reached its limit. "Really, Serena," she scolded, "this jealousy of Clara's good fortune is most unbecoming. I know that a London season is something that every girl desires, but you are not helping your situation by fretting."

"I'm not jealous." But there was no conviction in my protest, for how could I deny her words without giving away the guilty truth?

My mother sniffed, and sent me out to visit an indigent family, perhaps to remind me of how much worse things could be. The Freemans had lived locally for many generations, but their situation had worsened with each year. Every spring there seemed to be less money and more mouths to feed, and I knew that without the support of my mother they would have struggled greatly. Despite that, they accepted help only grudgingly, and visiting their cottage was one of my least favourite pursuits. That morning, however, I was glad to get out to feed my misery and desire for Clara without criticism, and I took the bundle of clothes without a single word of complaint.

By the time I returned, it was mid-afternoon, and I walked into the house to find Mama and Father deep in discussion.

"It can't be thought of," Mama was protesting. "Think of the clothes she would need, not to mention the transport costs!"

"It seems that it has been thought of," Father replied calmly. "And with such a generous offer from Lady Maria, I feel that it would be discourteous to refuse. After all, we have the clothes, in the main, already."

The conversation trailed off as my parents noticed my presence.

"What has Lady Maria done?" I asked. My heart beat fast with a hope that I dared not even admit to myself.

My mother pursed her lips. "Did you take those clothes to the Freeman's?" she inquired, changing the subject quickly.

I was tempted to retort that I had left them in a field, but the expression on my mother's face suggested that this was not the moment for impertinence. "Yes, Mama."

"And is the family keeping well?"

That was a more difficult question to answer. The small daughter had a serious cough, but Mr. Freeman had refused to allow me into the cottage, and had sent Germaine to the corner of the room, out of my sight. Although he was prepared to accept the warm garments, he did not brook any interference with his family. I was torn between the easy lie—that everything seemed fine—and my own fears for their little girl. "I don't know," I said at last.

Mama frowned. "How so?"

"Germaine's cough does not seem to be improving," I explained. "But Mr. Freeman would not allow her near me."

Mama's frown grew deeper. "She has been coughing for some time now," she said anxiously. She turned to Father. "I think I will have to pay them a visit myself."

"And about..." Father gestured, a letter in his hand.

"Later, Horace." And my mother was gone.

* * *

Several days later, on Friday, to be specific, I discovered for certain the subject upon which my parents had been deliberating. Mama told me to come into her room and I settled myself in the armchair beside her bed.

"It seems, Serena, that you are a luckier girl than perhaps you deserve to be." I looked confused, and Mama's face lightened a little. "Well, perhaps not. You are a good girl, after all," she said consolingly.

"Thank you," I murmured. I wondered both what had brought her to that conclusion after her oft-repeated scoldings for my dreaminess, and—more strongly still—when she would get to the point. Was it—could it possibly be that I might get to see Clara again? Were her parents bringing her back for another ball in the country, or (oh, dangerous fantasy!) might I get to visit my darling in London? However much my brain pointed out how improbable it was that Lady Maria would have invited me, my heart could not help but hope.

"Lady Maria wrote to your father and me not two days ago," Mama continued. "She suggested that you might, perhaps, like to go on a visit to London."

I gasped. "Are you sure?" I didn't mean to doubt Mama, but I knew how little Lady Maria approved of my friendship with Clara. It seemed almost too wonderful to believe that she really had invited me. "She truly has asked me?"

I stood up, unable to keep my seat in my excitement, and although my mother's smile was a little dubious, I could see that she liked my enthusiasm.

"I was not certain, myself, whether it would be appropriate to allow you to go, but your father says that the offer is most unexceptionable. He thinks that a short while in the bustle of London will not harm you."

I knew what my mother was thinking. I could see in her eyes her anxiety that my head would be turned by the balls and socialising of my weeks in town, and that I might come back even less fit for my everyday tasks than I presently was. Little did she know that it was neither the balls, nor even the change in my everyday life that I looked forward to, but to being with Clara once more. Just to be in her company once again would be wonderful. But of course, I could share little of these thoughts with Mama. In her innocent eyes, Clara and I were merely friends—and so her impression needed to stay.

"I may go, then?"

She nodded. "Yes, you may go."

"Tomorrow?" I asked eagerly, and she laughed.

"Soon."

Of course, nothing could be arranged as quickly as I would have liked. There were, after all, the dresses which had been put away to bring out and organise. Letters must be written to accept the invitation, transport must be arranged; a thousand and one little details must be organised…

One day followed another, more painfully slow than ever; but I reminded myself each night that each day that passed was a day closer to Clara. And finally, not much over a week since my mother had spoken to me, on the twelfth day of April—just over a month since I had last seen my love—I was on my way, travelling to London.

CHAPTER FIVE

April

I think Lady Maria approved of the calm reserve of my reunion with Clara. In earlier days we had been reprimanded for dashing at each other as soon as we met, both talking at once. But now, fearful of showing too much, I found myself almost incapable of speech at all. Especially when Clara looked so suddenly grown up, in her morning dress of light, rosy pink. Her wardrobe was almost totally new for her season, and had been chosen with care by Lady Maria, who excelled at selecting dresses that showed off her daughter to best effect. The gown for the coming out ball, it seemed, had been no lucky choice but the first statement of intent by Clara's mother. Everything about Clara, from her clothes to her demeanour seemed to scream, "Look at me: I am young, attractive, wealthy, eligible…" It was as if my friend had disappeared beneath the weight of family expectation.

"Hello," I said shyly.

"Good day, Serena," Lady Maria said. "I trust your journey was comfortable?"

Still Clara did not speak. I replied, "Oh yes, thank you. It was not as long as I was expecting."

"And your family, they are well?" she asked, sounding as if she hoped they were not.

"Yes, thank you."

I looked again at Clara, who was unnaturally silent, and the smile she gave me reassured me a little. It was just as I remembered it—bright, teasing, loving. Although she walked across the room with a cultivated, slow tread that seemed unlike her, her face told me that she was not so very much changed underneath. The sparkling eyes, the big, happy smile—these were all still there.

"Serena, what a pleasure to see you!" The small wink she gave me out of sight of her mother encouraged me further.

"I am glad to have come." I turned to Lady Maria. "I am so very grateful to you for the invitation."

Lady Maria inclined her head slightly in place of an answer. "Clara, perhaps you could show Serena to her room."

"Yes, Mother."

I glanced at my friend and wondered about her unusual docility, but she walked to the door and ushered me out without another word. We moved silently up the elegant staircase, its banisters adorned with carved wooden roses, and entered my bedchamber. Clara shut the door behind us. Then, she flung herself luxuriously across the bed, and laughed.

"Oh, the pressure! I do not know how much longer I can keep this facade up. And your face, Serena! Did you wonder whether I had been replaced by a statue?"

I laughed with her. "You're not so very changed, I see."

"No. No," she said again, as she sat up. Her face took on a little more seriousness. "Underneath, dearest, not changed at all."

For a moment, we looked at each other, strangely shy after our weeks apart.

"Clara?" I whispered.

"As ever," she said. She took my hand in hers and raised it to her lips, kissing each finger in turn. "Oh, I have missed you."

I could feel a tingle where her kisses touched my skin, reminding me how much I had longed for her. I thought of what it had been like without her at home, how I had often looked up in the hope of seeing her when I was out in the village, only to remember once more that she had gone away. I thought of the nights, when I'd dreamed of her—when I'd dreamed that we were holding each other, touching, kissing. "I have missed you, too."

I sat down on the bed beside her, and we turned to each other, needing the comfort, the reassurance—the reminder that neither of us had changed our minds about the love we shared. The kiss was clumsy but as we drew apart, I knew that Clara was mine still, no matter what had happened since we last met.

"Come closer," Clara murmured. "Please? I want to—oh Serry, I don't even know what it is I want to do, save that I can't do it without you."

I understood what she meant. I, too, had experienced that longing which only Clara could assuage. My arms were around her in seconds. We clung close—close—closer, and tiny trails of lightning flickered through my body. My heartbeat was as loud as thunder. Our kisses grew more confident, less clumsy. In time we were both shaking; it was only with difficulty that we pulled away, rearranging our clothes and hair.

"I'm sorry, my love," Clara said. "I don't know what's come over me! I didn't mean to do that. I was so full of good intentions. But Serry, I couldn't help myself."

"I needed you so badly," I confessed. I stood up. It was too hard to think with Clara so very close. I walked away a few paces and we smiled at each other in tremulous joy from either side of my bedchamber.

"I'm so glad you're here," said Clara softly.

"Not as glad as I. And indeed, it was very generous of your mother to offer to have me here," I added. "I don't think a letter has ever so surprised me!"

Clara grinned wickedly. "Wasn't it stunning? And so very unlike Mother, too."

I had not liked to say that, and my suspicions were now roused. "Whatever do you think possessed her? What are you not telling me?" I demanded. "Is there something…?"

"Oh, Serry. Silly, innocent Serry. You surely don't believe my mother wished to invite you? I half-suspect that among her ambitions for London was a determination to get me out of the corrupting influence of your family—especially, I believe, your mother, with her fawning interest in the lower classes!"

"Then how...?"

The grin settled into a smug smile. "Father. I caught him in his study one day when Mother was out on a morning call. I recounted a three-volume melodrama about how sad it was that his best friend's daughter had no chance to see the sights of London even if only for a week or two." She pulled a woebegone face to demonstrate. "'Poor Serena, when I have everything and she has nothing. Father, isn't there something we can do for her?' Bless him, the darling, he took the hint beautifully, and my mother's letter was written within the week." She reached out and squeezed my hand. "And you're here. You're here," she sang, as she leapt to her feet and performed an impromptu dance. "Oh, Serena, how I've missed you!"

I laughed again, unreservedly happy. This was my Clara, my love. She had shed the cool, elegant manners of the parlour and was her own self once more, vital and spirited.

"Tell me all that's happened. You at least have had new interests," I said. "I've been at home, my mother telling me ten times a day that I need to do more and dream less."

"Whereas mine has told me just the opposite: 'Clara, sit still.' 'My dear, don't fidget.' 'Clara, my dear, present a dignified reserve.'" She sat down again on the bed, and the mattress bounced beneath her weight. She looked ruefully at me. "You're right, of course—it has been new and exciting. I'm surprised I have not burst with the struggle to keep it all inside me. But whenever I've been tempted to yell my delight, I've thought about you and how much I wished you were by my side. Having had the presentation together, it hasn't seemed right going to engagements without you."

"Home isn't home without you, either."

Home. Home had *always* meant Clara, for as long as I could remember. When either of us had been away in the past, we had both written a calendar, charting the days until we were back; we crossed them off, one by one. I had not had the heart to do it for the season—too many days were due to pass before I could possibly hope to see my best friend. My best friend and lover—for how much more I'd missed her now, even than I had in the past. We made each other whole.

Clara sat back beside me and took my hand again between both of hers.

"But now you're here! And now, life really can begin."

The next days were dizzy with dissipation. Rout parties, balls, afternoon visits, riding in the park (where the intent was not so much to ride as to *be seen* riding), shopping—all these things tumbled over each other in a display of decadence and overindulgence, so that the question each day was not whether we had just one social obligation to go to, but which of the many we might choose. Lady Maria was in her element. She made certain that Clara (and, by default, I) went to the most highly regarded occasions, by which she usually meant those with the highest number of titled attendees. When at the events themselves, however, she knew better than to push Clara upon the notice of important people. She did not need to; Clara's vivacity, even toned down to her mother's satisfaction, made her popular, and Lady Maria knew better than anyone that her relations and financial status would stand up to the most pressing examination of the *ton*. There might have been problems persuading polite society to accept Clara's impoverished friend, but once again the high regard in which my Aunt Hester was held came to my assistance, and I was received everywhere.

On my second day in London, I joined Clara for the obligatory morning ride. Born and brought up in the country, I had ridden as long as I could remember, and the meandering pace required by town etiquette bored me dreadfully. With Lady Maria out with us, even the conversation was dull. We were allowed to discuss only the most trivial commonplaces. Clara, too, found little entertainment in this prim parade, which rarely moved from a walking pace.

We had just begun to trot for the first time when Clara drew her horse up short.

"Oh," she gasped, eyes gleaming with fascination. "Look! Serena, just look. Wouldn't it be—wouldn't it be simply marvellous to have one of those?"

We nudged our mounts to the side of the path as a lady drove herself past in a high perch phaeton. I smiled. I could so very much imagine Clara dashing about behind a fine pair of horses, dressed in the highest kick of fashion, her face lit up with enjoyment. But any reply I might have offered was cut short by Lady Maria.

"Disgraceful," she said severely, her lips pinched together in disapproval. "You would hardly like to be considered *fast*, Clara, and really that turnout can be described in no other terms."

"No, Mother," Clara agreed. She tore her eyes reluctantly away from the young lady, whose speed was certainly fast, whether her behaviour might be considered so or not.

For the first time in my life, I found myself grateful when the ride came to an end.

After our return to the Battersley's house, we took tea in the drawing room, and waited for any visitors who might choose to pay a morning call. Clara's mind went back to the elegant lady we had seen. She murmured to me, "But it did look thrilling, Serena, didn't it? That phaeton, and the matching pair? And surely it cannot be so very inappropriate, with a groom up behind one? Mama is so old-fashioned!"

"I suppose it is better to be too strict than not strict enough," I suggested doubtfully.

"Yes," Clara sighed. "But anything would be more interesting than that dreary morning ride."

Other parts of the social scene appealed to us more. I enjoyed the dance parties, where Clara and I and some of the other debutantes practised our steps so that we would be movement perfect at evening entertainments.

Although I had not Clara's vivacity to aid my progress (nor, indeed, her wealth), I soon began to hold my own within the social whirl. Having Clara with me gave me confidence, and in the days and nights that followed, I began to recognise faces and names; the bustle did not seem quite so terrifying as it had felt at first. My lack of fortune prevented me from being seen as of marriageable potential by many gentlemen, but as I had as little interest in them, I did not see this as an insurmountable problem. I was certainly not shunned, and as long as I might enjoy myself—dance a little, chat and giggle with Clara and certain others of the debutantes, and watch from the sidelines the jockeying for position of the acclaimed belles of the year—I was more than content with my lot.

The first "official" event I attended was a ball, held by Sir Walter James and his wife. It was rather hot and very crowded, but so gay and full of life that it was impossible to dislike it. There was laughter and gossip, and the most beautiful dresses I had ever seen. To my utmost delight, I encountered my cousin Anna there. As the music suffused the hall with a jaunty rhythm, she danced up to me—almost literally—and dragged me across to meet her partner, a tall young gentleman.

"This is Charles," she said, a possessive pride in her voice. She slipped her arm through his. "We're engaged. Charles, this is my cousin, Serena."

"Congratulations!" I said. Mama's suspicions about Anna's likely betrothal had been correct, I noted with amusement.

"Thank you," said Charles. "And now, Anna," he chided my cousin teasingly, "perhaps you might introduce us properly. I can hardly go around calling your cousin by her first name. People will wonder to which of you I am engaged!"

I laughed. Looking at Charles, it was clear to see that he was as besotted with Anna as she with him; no one would have a moment's doubt as to which of us was his love.

Anna's eyes twinkled. "Oh well," she said, taking on an air of mock-grandeur. "Miss Coleridge, this is Mr. Grey. Mr. Grey, pray let me present Miss Coleridge to you. Miss Coleridge and I are first cousins, you may be interested to know."

He bowed politely to me. "Miss Coleridge," he said, taking his tone from his betrothed, "it is indeed an honour to meet you."

"And I, you." My curtsey was equally formal, though all of us shared the amusement.

I had known from my mother's reports that Mr. Grey was both rich and respectable; nevertheless, this was most certainly a love match. It made me happy to see Anna and him together. I saw many married and betrothed couples in my time in London, but none who seemed so perfectly in harmony. Anna's betrothal, however, did not serve to make her neglectful of her young country cousin. She often introduced me to this or that lady, and although Mr. Grey invariably greeted me ironically with a formal bow, his smile was far more genuine.

I knew full well that Lady Maria saw my well-respected relations as the most acceptable thing about me, and I was grateful for Anna's good-natured support, I took the first possible opportunity to introduce her to Lady Maria.

"Lady Maria, please allow me to present my cousin, Miss Carlton, and her fiancé Mr. Grey."

Anna smiled and curtseyed; Mr. Grey produced a most creditable bow. Lady Maria very nearly unbent enough to smile, and it was evident in the way I was treated by Clara's mother for the next few days that she was impressed by my connections. Anna, however, held no such reciprocal high opinion, though she was polite enough not to say in words how little she liked my hostess. She rolled her eyes at the mention of Lady Maria's name, and the regular subtle ways in which she tried to make up for what she saw as the Awful Ordeal of Living with the Battersleys, demonstrated how she felt. She always ensured that I had partners at the balls and routs, sent me flowers to wear as a corsage from time to time, and always—but always—introduced me to the most important people in the *ton* before Lady Maria had a chance to do so. Considerably more regrettably, Anna was not overfond of Clara, either. Both of them vivacious and outgoing girls, they yet seemed to rub each other the wrong way on a regular basis. I think Anna felt that some of Clara's gaiety was forced, with the intent of putting me in the shade. And I know that my cousin watched my friend with hawk-like eyes for any suggestion that she might patronise me in the same way that Lady Maria did. In return, Clara's normal high spirits were blighted slightly in Anna's presence, thus adding weight to my cousin's suspicion that her exuberance was manufactured rather than natural. It was a pity, but with so many of my wishes fulfilled—London, Clara, dancing, balls—I did not spend too much time repining. And at this, my very first ball, the minor issues had not come to a head. Anna introduced me to many of her friends, my dance card was full, and I was with Clara. I do not think I could possibly have been happier.

In between the hubbub of the season's activities, Clara and I managed to find some time to spend together, alone—swapping secrets of the soul and the body. Often in theory we were supposed to be "resting," each in her own bedchamber; in practise, however, we found it possible to curl up together in her or my room, and enjoy the restfulness and serenity of each other's company. We rediscovered our delight in our physical relationship. I felt more certain than ever that no man could possibly live up to the pleasure I found in Clara. She was, at once, so familiar and so exciting that the only cloud on my horizon was that my visit would at some point end, and we would be parted again. No specified time for my return to the country, however, had as yet been spoken of; although Clara had only pleaded with her father to allow my visit for a week or two, he was far too fond a father to place such strict limits on her pleasure. Clara and I, therefore, chose to ignore the shadow of our parting and revelled in the moments we had.

CHAPTER SIX

May

Perhaps we got too confident. I do not know. One Tuesday afternoon, after we had spent the morning purchasing those garments of which we were most in need (silk stockings, in Clara's case; a new pair of evening gloves for me), we slipped away, as we had so often done, to Clara's room. Clara shut the door with a careful quietness, and pressed a teasing kiss to my lips.

"And now, my darling, come here."

She sat down on the bed, holding her arms out to me; an invitation I had no intention of turning down.

"Clara, oh Clara!" I could not deny that I loved the balls, the excitement and gaiety that London had to offer. But I lived—really lived—for moments like this, when Clara and I were alone and I could gather her in my arms and pull her close, or snuggle up to her warm, giving body.

"Serena." Clara ran her hand through the long strands of my hair, undoing in seconds the hour's work that had been put into restraining my locks by my maid. "Serena, I do love you so."

My head rested on her shoulder and I kissed her neck over and over. Clara fell backward across the bed, and dragged me down on top of her; she tugged my hair in order to direct my mouth to hers. We kissed, kissed, *kissed* as if the world held nothing but each other, as if we were free to love as well and as much as we liked. The universe had shrunk to the size of Clara's bed; all that mattered to me was there, as our dresses rustled against one another, and I delved into the pleasures of Clara's mouth.

Clara's warm fingers ran gentle paths over my shoulders. She put her mouth to the lobe of my ear and whispered heated words of encouragement—"Yes, Serena, darling, oh please, yes"—as I sought the buttons of her dress and undid them one by one, less clumsy at the task than I had once been. She smelt of flowers—roses and violets—and I pressed my face against her skin to breathe in the scent of her. Clara wriggled beneath me, trying to untangle herself from the restrictions of her primrose yellow dress, and I moved away enough to allow her to struggle free. But as soon as she had, she put her arms out and tugged me back to her, so that I lay almost covering her on the bed. I felt the softness of her breasts against my body, heard her making soft noises of pleasure as she tangled her legs and arms around me, holding us together. I delved deep, deeper, into her mouth with my tongue, one hand behind her head.

We were consumed in each other—too consumed to hear the sound of the opening door. It was not until a voice spoke that I realised we were no longer alone. A hand grabbed at the back of my dress, and I felt the flimsy material tear as I was pulled ferociously away from Clara. "What is this? What is this perversion?"

The hand dropped from my clothing as if the very touch had burnt, and I caught my first glimpse of Lady Maria as I turned. Her face was burgundy, and as I leapt to my feet, I caught the terrifyingly angry expression on her face.

"How *dare* you?" Her voice was not the voice I was used to. All her precepts of serenity and gentility seemed forgotten. She was spitting in her fury, her tone harsh. She caught my arm and dragged me painfully away from Clara. When my eyes met my love's, I saw Clara was green—white; her eyes seemed several sizes too large for her face. Clara, in all other circumstances so brave, was a different girl with her mother: cowed, her personality stifled. And the present situation was enough to intimidate anyone. But it was not to Clara that Lady Maria spoke, but to me. "How dare you come here and corrupt my daughter?" she demanded.

I was silent. I was not certain I would ever speak again. Clara's eyes filled with tears as she tried to protest.

"Mother!"

"Silence," Lady Maria snapped.

Her grip on my arm tightened so much that I winced with pain, and she thrust me out of the room and into my own. The colour in Clara's mother's face had not subsided: she looked uglier than I could ever have imagined possible, a veritable ogress. I wanted to push her away and run back to Clara, to take Clara in my arms and promise my undying love. Lady Maria had spoiled everything we had, making it seem as grotesque as she now appeared. I had never known hatred, but I think I hated her in that moment.

She spoke again. "You will return home in the morning," she said curtly. "Until then, you will not leave this room."

She left immediately and slammed the door behind her. A second later, I heard the metallic snap of the key as it turned in the lock. At any other time, I would have been furious at this mistrust, but now my heart was too full of anguish. As I stood by the open window, I could hear the angry tones of Lady Maria's voice as she spoke to Clara. Clara's replies (if indeed she made any) were too quiet to perceive. But I heard the moment when Lady Maria stalked out of Clara's room, and I heard Clara sobbing.

I could not cry. I could not cry. This pain was too severe for tears. I went to the window and looked out at the busy street below, and wondered if this was how it felt to die.

* * *

The night was long and sleepless. My emotions were too raw to allow me any type of rest, whether mental or physical. Three of Lady Maria's maids had been sent up to my chamber to pack my clothes away; she had clearly forbidden them to speak to me, but I cared little. I did not want to talk to anyone. I almost rushed forward to stop them, though, as they tugged my dresses roughly from the wardrobe. That blue one…I had been wearing that when I arrived, when Clara and I met again for the first time. I watched as a maid folded it carelessly and thrust it into my box. Not content with forbidding them to speak—or, it seemed, even to look at me, Lady Maria had evidently ordered speed above carefulness, and the maids had taken her at her word. Another dress, sprigs of green leaves decorating the white muslin. I remembered Clara undressing me so slowly from it, kissing me time after time.

Clara, oh Clara! Her weeping had continued for more than an hour before dissolving into long sobbing breaths. Shortly after the maids left me, I heard her door open and her mother order her downstairs. I wondered whether I too would be summoned, but instead a plate of cold food was brought up to my room by one of the stony-faced maids. She placed it on the dresser before she left, and locked the door once more. The food was scant, but it did not matter. It might have been champagne and quail, and I still would not have been able to eat a mouthful. It lay untouched.

Several times during the night, I heard Clara crying once more. It hurt—both that I could not comfort her, and that I was the cause of her grief. If it had not been for me…

Dawn broke slowly. I listened to the sounds of London town waking; I heard the maids come down from the attic to begin their day's work. I had not changed for bed, so I was still clothed in the same torn dress of yesterday, crumpled and uncomfortable. I wondered if I were to be delivered to the carriage still wearing it, but at length Lady Maria unlocked my door, nodded to a maid to deposit a pail of water on the floor, and with a minimum of words encouraged me to wash and change.

"The maids left you a dress, I think." Her tone was cold; it was almost a relief after the previous day's hot rage. I opened the wardrobe and saw that there was, indeed, one dress still hanging there—lonely, like myself. "And there will be a new shift and petticoat in the drawer. You have ten minutes until I return."

My washing was, I fear, perfunctory. I found I could not care enough to be thorough. I was glad of the new dress, however—I could hardly bear to look at the one I had taken off, loaded as it was with memories of horror. It took only seven minutes until I was ready for the journey. I sat on the edge of my bed, and waited for Lady Maria. I had but one question I both dreaded and needed to ask her.

The sound of the key in the door was loud across the silence of my room.

"The carriage is below," Lady Maria announced. She saw my discarded garments on the floor and added, "The maids will burn these."

I summoned up my courage. "Will you tell my parents?" I both feared and hoped that she would, as I knew not how to explain myself to them.

Lady Maria did not reply, but instead ushered me before her, prisoner-like, to the carriage. She offered me no breakfast. I saw no one else from the house—not Clara, not her father or brother, not even another of the maids. If I had needed any further demonstration of how disgraced I was, this deliberate shunning was proof enough. It was almost a relief to be going home—except that I hated not only to leave Clara, but to leave her without a word. I looked up at the window of her room as the carriage drew off, and wondered whether it was wistful imagination which made me see a pale, wan face looking down at me.

I had no idea how I was going to explain to my mother the reason for my premature return. I spent most of the miserable, achingly long journey torn between the agony of being parted between Clara and the fear of what I should say to my parents. As it turned out, however, I had no need to say anything.

I clambered down from the carriage, stumbling a little with the stiffness of the long journey, and walked toward her. Since

Lady Maria had caught us the previous night, I felt as if I had swallowed something too large for my throat. Now, as I made my way toward my mother, it seemed that someone had filled my boots with lead.

It seemed that Lady Maria, not content with banishing me to my bedchamber until the morning, had spent the rest of the evening composing a long and vitriolic epistle to my parents. She had sent it immediately; it had preceded me by almost an entire day. I did not need telling of the letter. One look at the white, set face of my mother told me everything: the details of Clara's and my behaviour had reached her.

She said nothing.

I don't know what I had expected—tears, recriminations, anger, perhaps—but the quiet immobility of Mama was more terrifying still. I did not know how to combat such a reaction. My own voice seemed caught below that lump in my gullet, unable to force its way into my mouth. In silence, Mama watched the coachman get down my cases; in silence saw the maid take them into the house. Then, finally, she spoke.

"Come in, Serena." I followed her into the house, and she led me upstairs to my room. Alice was beginning to unpack for me, but my mother gestured her away. "Later, please."

Heaven knew what story was going around the servants' quarters about my unexpected return. I probably ought to have cared, but all I could think about was the fact that Clara and I had been separated, probably forever, and that my usually calm and practical mother looked on the point of swooning.

"I'm sorry," I whispered when we were alone.

Mama leaned against the door of my room, her hands clenched by her sides. I willed myself not to bawl like a tiny child.

"Please, Serena, tell me it isn't true," she said.

It was a reassurance I could not give. "I'm sorry," I said again.

My mother walked to the window and looked out. I think she could not face me as she spoke.

"I received a letter from Lady Maria this morning," she said tonelessly. "In it, she informed me that you have been corrupting her daughter, attempting to ruin all of her chances of a good marriage with your perverted practices. She said…" My mother choked, and it was a moment or two before she could continue. "She said that she caught you kissing Clara in a fashion that could not be seen as sisterly. Clara, it seems, had no choice but to…" Mama cut off again, visibly steeling herself for what she had to say, "…to accept what you forced upon her."

Do hearts break? It felt as though mine shattered in a second to hear our relationship, our beautiful, incredible love, described in such a fashion. To hear myself accused not only of what was true—kissing my dearest friend—but also of that which was not—that I forced myself, or would ever force myself upon her. It was a mixture of truth and untruth so closely entwined as to be almost impossible to disentangle. And, after all, what good would it do to deny?

I *had* kissed Clara; I had done much more than that, if truth be known. I had made love with her time and time again, and though I had known that others would see it as wrong, I could not believe that anything so magical and true could be a sin. I still could not believe it, even with the sight of my mother's shaking back as she tried to control her emotions in front of me. What was more, Clara had wanted me to kiss her, to touch her. She had revelled in our passion as much as I. It had been no sordid liaison.

I opened my mouth to defend myself, and then shut it again. How would it help if I told Mama that Clara had been as much involved as I? My life was in pieces; what good would it do to ruin hers also? Biting my lip until it bled, I realised that protecting Clara's reputation would probably be the last thing I could ever do for her.

Mama stood by the window a while longer, seemingly waiting for me to speak, but there was nothing to say. Clara was lost to me. What did it matter in comparison what others thought of me, what they thought me capable of? Even for the sake of my parents, I could not soften the blow.

"Very well," Mama said flatly. "I see there is no more to be said. I will send your supper up to your room. I must talk with your father."

She opened the door quietly, and left. The tears which had refused to come the previous night, when I had heard Clara's heartbreak, arrived now that I was in the safety and familiar comfort of my own room. The room was as it ever had been, only I had changed. I felt strangely apart from myself. I walked to the mirror and looked at the girl there, her cheeks stained with wetness, her face pale and drawn. I told myself that I was that girl; but it seemed difficult to comprehend. Was it really barely more than a day since Clara and I had giggled and chattered with the other debutantes at the luncheon party? And now…I would probably never see Clara again.

Perhaps for the first time, I faced the true meaning of a future without Clara. It was then that I wept in earnest, big, gut-wrenching sobs that brought me to the point of sickness. I almost did not have time to take a breath before the next wave of emotion hit me. Abandoning every thought save one—that Clara was lost to me—I lay on the floor and cried out my heartbreak.

* * *

My mother came to me. I had put her through so much in the way of shame and embarrassment, yet she still could not leave her daughter to weep alone. Her arms were around me; she pulled me up so that I sat propped by my bed, and she wiped my eyes with the gentleness she had shown to me when I was a small child and I'd hurt myself. I clung, and sobbed, and she whispered comforting nonsense to me, hushing my crying until I was calmer. Even then, I could not prevent tears from rolling down my cheeks, and my mother stayed for most of the night. She said little but warmed me by her presence. I was relieved that I had not been altogether cast off.

The next morning, however, we spoke again on the subject of my behaviour in London.

"I will not mention it again after this," Mama said, as we sat alone in the inner drawing room, "but there are some things I must say."

"Yes." I dug my nails into the palms of my hands in an attempt to prevent myself from weeping again. I owed it to my mother to listen with dignity. I did not want to upset her any more than I already had.

"Your father," Mama began. She steadied her voice with effort. "He is...distressed by this indiscretion, Serena. As you know, his friendship with Mr. Battersley is of long-standing, and he fears that your behaviour cannot help but damage that relationship, perhaps fatally."

"I'm sorry," I whispered.

"But it's more than that." Mama's self-control failed, just for a second. "He is—he can't—he would not disown you, you know that, but he—we..." She took a deep breath. "We can't understand how something like this could happen. I ask myself what we must have done wrong in your upbringing that you would come to this."

"It wasn't anything you did." I stumbled over the words. "It just...happened."

"You must understand that it will take your father and me a little time to recover, Serena. You are our daughter, and we love you. But we need time to come to terms with what has happened. Time to reflect. This is not easy for us, you know, but with God's help we will manage. And now," she said with a weak smile, "we will speak no more of it."

CHAPTER SEVEN

June-September

Mama kept her word. Since the first day after my abrupt return from London, Clara's name was never mentioned in our house. I knew that after a brief period of coldness, my father met with Clara's father still, but nothing ever was said. Unable to forget my indiscretion, my parents had expunged every mention of the Battersleys from conversation. It was, within our house, as if they did not exist.

I didn't care. Whether her name was said aloud or not, I missed Clara with tearing, agonising strength. I lay in bed and thought of her, and when I finally slept, my dreams were full of her. Sometimes we lay in each other's arms, and kissed as we once did; but in other dreams she stood accusingly before me, crying out. "*Why did you force me, Serena? Why did you catch me up in your unnaturalness? Why could you not leave me alone?*" I would wake in tears, and wonder if I knew what had really happened in London.

The pain did not diminish in the weeks that followed, but I learned to live with it. My father slowly grew able to be in my company without evident disgust; my mother made commonplace conversation—almost, she almost treated me as she once had. I was docile and obedient, and did as I was asked; eager for errands to run, where once I would have attempted to escape my duties. Anything, I would have done anything to keep me from my thoughts.

During these days I visited the poorer families in the village, and in particular saw a great deal of the Freemans, whose daughter's cough had caused such distress a few months earlier. Germaine had not recovered from her illness, and for a long time we feared for her life. My mother had paid for the doctor's visits, and therefore even Mr. Freeman had accepted her right to check on his daughter's health. But usually it was I who went down to the cottage, bearing food. It was an arduous journey, and my servant and I took turns carrying the heavy pot of broth which was Mama's staple offering.

I knew Alice had family in the village, so when possible, I encouraged her to visit them whilst I spent a half hour sitting with the Freeman family before starting the walk home. Occasionally, I took the newspaper, for Mr. Freeman enjoyed looking through it, and he was extremely proud of his ability to read confidently; he felt his skill set him a step above others in the district. One night, as I spooned soup up to little Germaine's mouth, he made a noise of surprise as he looked through the pages of that week's paper.

"Huh. Old Battersley's done the job then," he commented. "Or, more probably, that dame of his."

"I beg your pardon?" The remark appeared to be aimed at me.

"Got his daughter hitched, ain't he?" He leaned forward over the broad newspaper page.

Germaine made a little noise of protest as my hand stopped in midair, the spoon halfway between the soup bowl and her mouth.

"Clara?" The name seemed almost rusty from disuse.

"Got herself engaged to a Lord, it seems," he nodded. He scanned the news item. "No mention of a date or anything, mind. But there it is, sure as black is black."

Hastily, I ladled a large mouthful of soup Germaine's way and then got up to look over Mr. Freeman's shoulder. It could not be true. It could not be. But it was.

Mr. Matthew and Lady Maria Battersley are pleased to announce the engagement of their daughter, Clara Anne, to Lord Routledge of Dunlock.

I read no further. I had no need to. Clara, oh Clara! She had been lost to me long before this notice, but it hurt so much to read the news of her engagement. She had forgotten me, then, or did not care. She had moved on, but I…I knew I never would. Tears threatened to overcome me, but I knew I must not cry in front of the Freemans. I fought with my emotions; it felt as if I had lost the ability to speak, and I knew also that I was shaking. I walked back to Germaine's side, and attempted to conceal my distress in the action. After a couple of deep breaths I was able to respond.

"I'm sure she will be very happy," I said mechanically, and I picked up the spoon once more.

Freeman grunted. "Her Ladyship's been angling for a great pairing since the girl was Germaine's age. None of your ordinary folk for *her* daughter. Well, I wish her joy of it."

I mumbled some sort of assent, and left as soon as I decently could. My mind churned as I went over the shocking discovery. Was it selfish of me to have expected her to stay true to me, rejecting all others for my sake? Had I really forced her—or at the very least, overpersuaded her—into unnaturalness when really she longed for the safety and acceptability of a gentleman's love and affection? Was Lady Maria correct, after all? I could not bear to go home, to face my parents, until I had had time to get over the first impact of this news. I sent Alice back alone, despite her disapproval and loudly voiced objections, and wandered into the countryside to walk and walk and walk. The trees were in bloom; the air smelled of flowers, just as Clara had. Everything I saw, heard, smelled brought her more vividly to my mind. We had cantered our horses across this field; we had fought a dragon (in the shape of her little brother) under that tree; we had whispered and giggled together everywhere. We belonged together—I thought we belonged, but I was wrong.

I had forced Clara. I had made Clara behave unnaturally. All she really wanted was a happy marriage to a respectable gentleman, and I had come close to ruining her life by my unwanted attentions. More frenzied walking, as a second voice spoke up in my head. No, it hadn't been like that. It hadn't. Clara loved me. It was she who had made that first movement to kiss me, in the days before our presentation. She had wanted me; she had loved me.

My pace slowed, and for the first time I was aware of the cool breeze. June was a fickle month; it teased me with sunshine only to offer rain showers or a cold wind the next moment. But then, how equally fickle was my so-called love, that she could transfer her commitment to someone else in so short a time? How could she possibly claim to have loved me if she could accept her first offer of marriage? Perhaps his title had turned her head: she had been seduced by the promise of a high position. But that didn't sound like the Clara I knew. Then again, if Clara could be engaged so quickly, so easily, clearly she was not the girl I'd thought I'd known. Maybe I *had* seduced her. The same thoughts, round and round in circles in my head until I was dizzy and exhausted.

When I came to myself, I realized that more than an hour had passed since I departed the Freeman's house. Reluctantly I turned for home, wondering how to explain my long absence to my parents.

When I got there, however, it was to face another shock. I walked in on a discussion of the prospective wedding, perhaps prompted by the same newspaper announcement I had seen. My father felt it his duty to go to the wedding, my mother her equal responsibility to stay with me. There was, of course, no talk of my attending the function, even had I desired such a thing. As, in the circumstances, I could think of nothing I could possibly hate more, I was only grateful that I might stay away. It was evident from my mother's face, that Clara's betrothal had been common knowledge to my parents for several days. Determined as they were never to mention her name in my presence, such information had been kept from me intentionally. Now, my mother looked anxious as she saw that I had heard.

"Serena..."

I had lost so much: all I really had left to me was my dignity. "It is all right, Mama. I know." I looked at Father, and added coolly, "Please send my congratulations to her on her success."

Then I left the room. The cloak of pride dropped from me as soon as I was alone, and I was left with a frozen feeling which was bone deep, an iciness which no warmth could melt away. Too numb to cry, for a long time I gazed out of my chamber window toward the house which would never more be Clara's home.

* * *

My melancholy over Clara's betrothal was dissipated not by the village pursuits with which I tried to fill my days, but by a matter of national importance. After we first got over the shock of Napoleon's escape from Elba, and my father had arranged his business interests as best he could in the circumstances, we settled back into our normal routines. Only those families with soldier sons and fathers thought much about what was going on across the channel in France. My own life had been turned so dramatically upside down I had quite forgotten there was any greater relevance to his escape. I was concerned only with my personal circumstances—a shameful thing to admit, I know, but I'm certain I was not alone. The Battle of Waterloo, however, brought the war back to the forefront of our minds.

I am sure no one will ever forget the day when the news of Wellington's victory came through. A carnival attitude enveloped Winterton village as everyone celebrated the defeat of the bogeyman Napoleon. In our house, however, a different mood prevailed. My father's face was sombre, and I saw tears in my mother's eyes as she read through the lists of casualties that filled the newspaper. Name after name after name, most of them young men cut down in their prime. My mother would look up every so often and repeat a name aloud.

"Cavendish—Henry Cavendish. His mother and I were presented together." Then, "Oh—*oh*. William Marshall. I danced with his father so many times." A half smile as she reminisced.

"He asked me to marry him, long ago. It might have been my son's name in here." And at this, the tears overflowed and spilled down her cheeks as she reached her hand out to me. "Thank God I've got you, Serena. I can't imagine how those poor parents must feel."

I ran into my mother's arms, and only realised my own distress when I felt my hand shake as I raised it to wipe the tears from her face.

"Mama, Mama," I said, over and over as her arms encircled my shoulders and she leaned her head in against mine.

"I couldn't survive losing you, Serena," she murmured.

"You won't," I promised, and we stayed there, holding each other, for a long, long time.

* * *

The next event of any great note was Clara's wedding. My father, sticking to the plans which he had decided upon before Waterloo, went up to London to attend the occasion. It was, I knew, to be a huge event: the people in Winterton could speak of little else for several weeks. I cultivated a distant smile and a polite phrase of agreement which I used whenever I was told how wonderful it was that Miss Battersley had made such a splendid match. I survived, I think, only by a certain rigid pride which demanded that I should not make my distress widely known.

"Miss Coleridge will be quite lonely without her dear friend," I overheard one woman say in the market.

The date of the wedding was September 13th. "Unlucky thirteen," several locals muttered. For me, the date mattered not. How could Clara have forgotten me so easily that she could form an engagement within two months of our separation—how? The villagers, however, were more preoccupied by the general disappointment that Clara was to be married in London, rather than in her own home church "as is proper," said Mr. Freeman sternly to me on one occasion. I suspect that it was this fact more than any other (date notwithstanding) which caused the firm conviction in the village that Lord or no Lord, the marriage would come to no good. I was torn between the virtuous part of myself which wanted Clara to find happiness wherever she could, and the hurt, bitter side which didn't see why I should be the only one to suffer.

My father said little on the subject of the wedding before he left. He had forgiven me my sins but could not forget them, and when I thought about the effect of Lady Maria's accusations on the friendship between himself and Mr. Battersley, I could not blame him. After so many years of closeness—when Clara's brother had even been named after my father—it must have been a huge shock for him to be told that I had so grievously assaulted Clara. Indeed, I could only be amazed and grateful that he had not disinherited me on the spot. When he had gone, my mother was equally taciturn on the subject; instead, with a false enthusiasm, she marshalled the household into a massive cleaning operation.

"In your father's absence," Mama said lightly, "it seems just the time for some housekeeping. It should have been attended to long since, but your father dislikes so intensely having the house in an uproar that I have allowed things to get quite out of hand."

Consequently, I spent the day of Clara's wedding sorting out the linen cupboard. The sheets were divided into piles of those in reasonable condition and those for whom a new life should be found as cleaning cloths. It was the type of mindless task that gave me all too much time to think about what was happening in London, but I knew that left to myself I would have moped alone in my room, more dejected still and without even the comfort of performing a useful task. At least when my mother found me surrounded by neatly folded linen, I felt that I was doing what little I could to atone for previous sins.

I thought more of Clara over the next few days, and knew that she would be on her honeymoon, and that the unknown Lord Routledge would be…but my thoughts broke down at that point. I could not bear to think of a strange man touching my Clara; the very idea made me almost physically sick. My father returned three days later, and said briefly that all had gone well and that he and his godson had embarked upon a couple of excursions. Indeed, he spoke more of the innocent diversions that he and his namesake had experienced together than he did of the wedding. I presume he deemed it a safer topic for conversation.

"Just like a boy," he said, as he smiled fondly, and described a trip to see the wild animals at the Exeter Exchange on the Strand. "Horace was overcome with excitement at the sight of an elephant. He almost died of joy when the beast used his trunk to take a sixpence from his hand! He far preferred that to the theatre, though since his mother insisted that we see a morality piece, I can't say I altogether blame him! Lady Maria never did have any idea of what children enjoy."

And with that line, he stopped short. The mention of Lady Maria brought back to all of us the memory of her letter detailing my sins. Any further comments on my father's trip to London were heard by my mother alone, and were not again mentioned in my presence.

Life was quiet for a while after the turmoil of Clara's wedding settled down. She had been, it seemed, a beautiful albeit serious bride. I remembered how well white had suited her at our coming out ball, and could well believe in her beauty. The country folk were mightily impressed by the marriage; it was difficult to speak to any of them without the subject of the wedding being broached. Now that the ceremony was past, they managed to forget the bad omens of which they'd spoken in the weeks leading up to the occasion. Still I forced myself to smile. I explained that my own ill health had prevented my attendance. If the villagers put down any sign of distress I might unintentionally have shown to that, I could only be grateful. Certainly many a woman sympathised with me that I had missed out.

"And you and Miss Battersley always such good friends, as well, ever since you were little lasses. Sure, I don't know how she could go through with it without you beside her."

Many such comments were made to me over the weeks that followed, but I never got used to them—of hearing so many people speak of the closeness, the *love*, which had existed between Clara and me. I had loved her so much, had believed that she loved me. And now, she was the wife of a Lord, and I a disgraced daughter confined to the village of my birth.

1816

CHAPTER EIGHT

January-February

Christmas was a sedate occasion. We went through the motions, but I think all three of us had our minds taken up with other concerns. But just after the New Year, my mother sat me down for an important conversation.

"Your father and I have been talking," she said quietly, "and we have come to an agreement."

"About the field dispute?" I asked. The Freemans and their nearest neighbours, the Lances, had been in bitter battle over which of them had rights to a certain patch of land. They described it as a field, although it was barely more than ten feet square. The squabble had divided the village, and my father had stated his determination to sort it out only that morning.

She smiled a little.

"No, dear—about you."

"Me?" I asked. "What about me?"

"We think that you should have your season."

The words were a shock. After the debacle of my time with Clara, I had intended never to visit London again. I looked mutely at my mother.

"We would have given you one before," she said, "as you know. But with the battles and the threat—well, you know all that. But now, the shares which looked worthless not a year ago have increased so much in value that we feel we can give you what you should have had."

"But…"

She took my hand and held it gently.

"We've already decided, Serena. You will have your season after all."

I cannot say that, this time around, the prospect of going to London had any appeal. On my all-too-brief sojourn there ten months previously, I had been a guest of the Battersleys. Although my parents had produced some appropriate clothing for my visit, compared to Clara I had been almost shabbily dressed, and with little money to pay for any extras I might require. This time, however, it was I who would have the beautiful clothes, the most perfect shoes and hats—and it was Dead Sea fruit. With resignation rather than pleasure, I went through all the rigmarole of dress fittings, the organisation of this accessory against that. I bore with it for the sake of my parents, my mother in particular, who refused to reject a daughter accused of (and worse, acknowledging) deviance. Instead, my parents allowed me to recover myself under their forgiving protection, and my gratitude for this was as great a driving force as any anticipation.

"Serena, darling," my mother said, one evening as we sat together in my bedroom and she brushed out my hair, "I want you to know that there is no knowledge in town about—" her voice wobbled a little— "about your previous misdemeanour. You must not fear that."

"Lady Maria did not tell?"

Mama took my hand, and I felt her fingers contract involuntarily at the mention of Lady Maria. "No." She hesitated. "She could hardly have exposed you without some shadow falling on Clara." *On Clara?* I wondered. *Or on Lady Maria herself?* Mama knew what I was thinking. "Lady Maria wanted Clara to marry well. It seems she has been successful in that aim," said Mama, rather more tartly than I was accustomed to.

"I'm glad," I said untruthfully as I curled my hair around my finger. If Clara had been there, I thought, with a stab of pain, she would have scolded me for the action.

I knew that my mother, too, wished me to marry—but her idea of success was rather different. She wanted me only to be happy with my husband. I knew now that her hope would ultimately be disappointed. Torn from Clara, I could not imagine anyone in her place.

Soon after my governess, Miss Bruce, left, Mama spoke to me about the joys of marriage. Love, of course, had been top, but she had spoken too of family, children, and of financial security. I regretted the fact that I would never have a daughter of my own, but I knew that my parents would always support me financially, no matter what. I would not marry where I could not love, and I did not think that I would ever forgive nor even comprehend how Clara had turned so quickly (and apparently so easily) to such a very different life.

"Yes." Mama smiled wanly. "I just wanted to tell you, darling."

"Thank you." I kissed her quickly, and blinked back the tears before they could leak down my cheeks. I was grateful for my mother's support, but there was one thing it didn't change. *I* knew. I knew all too well what had happened; I was aware of my difference, aware that I bore a scar, albeit not a visible one.

I pressed my fingernails hard into my palms and forced myself for the first time to think of Clara as she now was. I didn't want to face the truth of her betrayal (for such I could not help but think it), but I needed to. I needed to forget my hurt, my anger, my longing, for when we met in town—a predictable occurrence, but one I dreaded—she would be Lady Routledge. She was no longer the Clara I knew—if, indeed, she ever had been. We would meet as acquaintances; ladies who knew each other merely through our families' long association, nothing more.

I prepared for my season joylessly, moving from dress fitting to deportment lessons, and looked forward only to seeing my aunt and cousin Anna again.

Aunt Hester was, of course, aware that I had stayed, for a few weeks, with the Battersleys last season. She accepted, however, without question, my mother's explanation that since Clara's marriage, both Clara and Lady Maria had been keen to drop the acquaintance. If my aunt thought Clara, as well as Lady Maria, outrageously high in the instep, such an impression was doubtless preferable to the truth. Anna's mild dislike of Clara helped along this impression. Anna had always suspected that Clara harboured her mother's haughtiness, and although unfair, her distaste was convenient in persuading my aunt that no more scandalous reason for the rupture in our friendship existed. And since the longer I could avoid either Clara or her mother the better pleased I would be, I was almost grateful to have this excuse to explain my anxiety. However, we would at some time meet, London society being what it was, and I dreaded our eventual encounter more than anything else.

At the first London ball I attended, I was terrified. Despite Mama's assurances, I felt certain the scandalmongers would only have to take one look at my face to have instant knowledge of my shameful past—or worse, that I would see Lady Maria or Clara, who knew the sordid details for certain. Of course, my fears were unfounded, as Lady Maria hadn't deigned to spread the news. Accompanied by Aunt Hester and Mama (an act of heroism by my mother, given her dislike of fashionable town life), I stood nervously at the edge of the room, prayed not to be noticed, and waited for the world to collapse around me.

It did not happen. As neither one of the prettiest nor one of the wealthiest ladies present, I was not precisely overwhelmed with attention, but that which I did receive was clearly not disapproving. Mama had been right, and no breath of scandal had escaped to the fashionable world. I danced more often than I stood and watched, though never when a waltz was played, of course. I had not been sanctioned to waltz and I had no wish to gain a reputation, however undeserved, for being "fast." I do not imagine I made much impression on the gentlemen with whom I danced, however—desperate not to be caught in any impropriety, I barely ventured a single comment of my own volition, and must have seemed almost unbearably insipid. Grateful when the event came to an end, I was thankful not to have shamed myself in any way.

* * *

Shortly after my first ball, my father, content that I was poised for success, returned home to tend to his responsibilities on the estate. My mother stayed a little longer.

"I want to settle you in, my darling," she said simply. "I have friends in town who will take to you for your own sake, but you're my only daughter, and I want to see you comfortable before I leave." She smiled. "I might not enjoy the season itself, but I have not been so foolish as to lose contact with all those I knew before my marriage. I knew that someday I would have a daughter to establish."

We therefore made morning calls to a number of old acquaintances, most of whom seemed entirely sincere in their pleasure to see my mother in town. Indeed, had she wished to reestablish herself, I was convinced she would have been able to do so with immediate effect. I did not do myself justice, as my shyness and anxiety overwhelmed my ability to converse well. However, I heard more than one of Mama's friends describe me as a "prettily-behaved young lady—not too pushing." It seemed my silence had made me appear well-bred rather than dull.

One of the ladies Mama made sure we visited was Lady Sefton. Mama had known her as a dashing young lady in the early years of her marriage; they had kept up a desultory correspondence. With Lady Sefton now acting as one of the famed Patronesses of Almack's, her association with my mother turned out to be highly useful. Lady Sefton's sincere, if mild, affection for my mother made her happy to give "dear Elizabeth's daughter" the sought after voucher for the famous club.

The second ball I attended—there had been dance parties and breakfasts between—was enlivened by an unexpected meeting with an old acquaintance: Mr. Feverley. He attended Lady Ratchett's ball with the air of someone horribly and uncomfortably out of place. He greeted me with a look of relief which was flattering; he evidently remembered our dance at my coming out ball more than twelve months previously. His stammer had not improved since we last met: his first remark, after a creditable attempt at "good evening" was "W-will you d-dance with me?" He smoothed down his ginger hair, and looked even more nervous than I.

I smiled at him. "Yes, please."

If his stammer had not improved, his dancing skills had. By the time we moved a few places down the line, we chatted like old friends. Feverley, once one got used to his speech impediment, was an interesting man. We swapped opinions of books, and Feverley made me laugh on several occasions with his gentle humour. At the end of the dance, I echoed Feverley's remark from our first encounter, and told him that this was the first dance I had enjoyed in London.

"You f-flatter me, Miss Coleridge," he said with disbelief, but by the time we parted, I had convinced him that my compliment was true.

We danced again before the end of the ball, and discovered with mutual pleasure that we were both due to attend Mrs. Elton's party later that week. Indeed, I venture to say that it was at that moment I had my first positive emotion toward London life. Up until then, I had seen the raft of obligations as an onerous duty, embarked upon to please my parents and to demonstrate that in some ways I was, indeed, the daughter they hoped for. Mr. Feverley, evidently, was under a similar obligation to satisfy his own mother. I did not know, and did not intend to ask, the nature of his indebtedness—money, I suspected—but we each saw in the other something we liked, and I hoped, despite my disinclination to find romance, I might at least make a friend. Feverley was not good-looking, and his manners, on the surface, were not particularly prepossessing, but underneath lay a decent gentleman, with a kind heart and excellent wit. I would be grateful to count myself his friend. What he saw in me, I did not know—I could only be glad that he did so. I confess it never occurred to me that we might be seen as a "couple"; I am equally sure it never occurred to Mr. Feverley.

Aunt Hester, however, although pleased to see that I had a friend, felt obliged to warn me.

"You do know, Serena, that Mr. Feverley's mother is notorious in social circles," she said gently. "She is, I regret to say, extremely underbred. Her manners and insistence that everyone take note of her social position leads only to recognition that she is vastly out of place in the *ton*. I try not to speak negatively of any lady, but Mrs. Feverley's pushing ways have made her infamous."

I panicked. "I do not damage my reputation by dancing and speaking with Feverley, do I?" The thought that I might commit yet another scandal—this time in public—was terrifying.

"No, no," she reassured me. She smiled fondly at my agitation. "But do not get taken in by him—or her."

I relaxed. "Believe me, Aunt Hester, I think he feels the same way about his mother as you, though he is too polite to say so!"

Aunt Hester laughed. "Then I shall say no more, Serena, and just be happy that you have met a friend."

Two days later, my mother returned to Winterton, leaving Aunt Hester and me to experience the highs and lows of the season without her. Mama was never happy when separated from my father, and I had seen for myself that each social occasion had been more trial than pleasure to her. She had been, in her day, if not an incomparable, then certainly a noted beauty. But she had been thankful to give a town life up and retire to the country after her marriage. Father and she made a perfect match in this: true country people at heart, who took pleasure in the simple pursuits which Winterton afforded them.

Aunt Hester, on the other hand, was the perfect companion for a life filled with social activities, and she was delighted to have another young person in her town house. She had been widowed five years, and since the marriage of Anna to Mr. Grey—a quiet affair, owing to a death in Charles's family—she had been predominantly alone. Knowing nothing of the contretemps surrounding my visit to London the previous year, she regarded me as a blessing—something which I hoped would last out the season.

Her older son Frederick, the present Lord Carlton, also lived in London, but preferred to leave the family house in Aunt Hester's hands whilst he lived in bachelor lodgings. I know my aunt hoped he would marry and reclaim the house, but he showed little sign of doing so as yet. Although we encountered him occasionally at events, it was the card room which enjoyed his patronage rather than the dance floor. His brother Edward was still attending Oxford; he'd passed his first exams with some success, and was working toward a further degree in mathematics. Aunt Hester was proud of him, if confounded by his enthusiasm for academic work. She saw in me, however, a surrogate daughter, and was extremely pleased to escort me to this and that social event. Whilst she had been justly pleased by Anna's marriage, she regretted the fact that she had no other daughters to launch. I came just in time, she told me regularly, to save her from her dotage.

A week later, the sword fell. My aunt and I were attending Almack's. *Everyone* who was *anyone* went to Almack's balls, if only to demonstrate they had the credentials to be admitted. I had not seen Clara since the moment that Lady Maria, incandescent with rage, had dragged me from her arms. It was one thing knowing it would happen, however; quite another to hear the announcement by the footman.

"Lord Routledge, Lady Routledge."

For a second, I felt if all my skin was on fire. I stumbled to a halt in my conversation, leaving poor Mr. Feverley visibly bewildered and anxious. No doubt he wondered what it was he had done wrong. I could vaguely hear him ask, "Sorry, did I…?"

I would see her in a moment. I would see her. I must not show my agitation—my anguish—my love. I forced myself to concentrate on Feverley.

"I'm sorry," I apologised. "I don't know what came over me." I looked desperately around the room for some convincing explanation.

"The heat, perhaps," Feverley said, and I clung to his suggestion.

"Yes, yes." I placed a gloved hand on my breastbone to quiet my heart.

"Perhaps a chair?" Feverley grasped my elbow and eagerly guided me toward the nearest chair, where I collapsed with more haste than grace.

"It is an awfully warm evening," Feverley said. He fluttered above me like an agitated moth. "Can I do anything for you, Miss Coleridge? A drink?" Even at the height of my distress, I was touched by his genuine concern for my well-being.

"Thank you."

I forced a smile. How strange that Feverley should always be present in my moments of deepest distress. I had danced with him when I had discovered the news of my father's financial collapse. Now, as I prepared for my first meeting with Clara since *that moment*, it was he who obediently trotted off to fetch me a drink for my supposedly overheated state. I watched him disappear and resolutely refused to allow my eyes to drift toward the entrance.

"Serena."

My fingers tightened instinctively on my reticule. *Her* voice. Clara. For a second I was not certain I could move, then with determination I looked up. Lord Routledge, a dark gentleman with eyebrows which almost met in the middle, had sauntered off to find himself a drink. It seemed that I was not important enough for his attention. I could only be grateful. Bad enough to be forced to speak to Clara, let alone to speak to her in the presence of the man who had cut me off from her forever. I knew my jealousy was unfair, and the worst of my bile was saved for Clara herself, who had forgotten me so quickly, but still I knew I could never forgive him.

But Clara—oh, Clara, who stood in front of me this moment. How could I bear to look at her, let alone force my voice to utter the pleasantries I knew I must offer?

"Good evening Clara—or Lady Routledge, as I gather I should say now." My voice was steady, and seemed utterly detached from my person, my very being. "I must offer you my congratulations."

I could not bring myself to look her in the eye.

"Serena." Clara's voice was beguiling and pleading at once. She sounded so much like *my* Clara, this woman who belonged to someone else entirely.

"You look well." I spoke by rote. I dared not look closely enough at her to judge her expression. But the dress she wore was beautiful, almost certainly of Parisienne making. It was a soft pink colour, and it shimmered around her in the flickering light, flowing to the floor like a waterfall of silk. I wanted to touch it—to touch her. I wanted to push her away and never see her again. It hurt, it hurt so much to be in her presence.

"Please, Serena, I—"

"Lemonade, Miss Coleridge?" Feverley was by my side again.

"Excuse me, Lady Routledge," I said politely, getting to my feet. "Thank you, Mr. Feverley."

I took the proffered drink from my squire, and walked with a purposeful air toward the other side of the ballroom as if I had an important engagement. Feverley trotted after me, bleating apologies.

"I say, I am so sorry. Wasn't that…wasn't she at that first ball? A friend of yours?"

"An old acquaintance." My heart was tearing itself into pieces. "Our fathers were…are…good friends."

"Oh. I thought…" I don't know what he saw in my face, but he trailed off, the sentence unfinished.

I forced a smile. "We were friends too, once—before her marriage."

Let him think our disagreement was over a man, that I was jealous that she had caught a Lord; let him think anything save the truth. No one must know about Clara's and my past, to save our reputations. If anyone ever found out about Clara and me, all chance of a life in London would be lost. My parents, even my aunt, would be shamed by their relationship with me. And in the eyes of Feverley—the one person with whom I had struck up a mild friendship—I would see disgust take the place of friendship, and be reminded once again of how deviant, how evil I was. An ever-ready blush suffused his face.

"I-I d-didn't mean to pry."

"I know." And my smile, if tremulous, was real now, not false. "That is why I told you." I glanced up, blinking rapidly. "The next dance is about to start. Don't you have a partner to attend?"

"Yes." He gave me a shy look. "Lady Jane Lawrence. My mother would be mortified if I offended her." He too was in the mood for confidences, it seemed. I had never known him so voluble. "May I dance with you again later? Or even," he added ruefully, "merely sit and talk? I am aware that my dancing leaves something to be desired."

I remembered once again how much I liked him, this gentleman who could so readily admit to his failings. There was an honesty about him which made me ashamed of my own secrecy.

"Your dancing is by no means as bad as you claim; it is only confidence that you lack. I would like that very much," I said, and with a brief bow, he left me.

CHAPTER NINE

March

As if it had not been difficult enough seeing Clara again, the event was followed less than a week later by my first meeting with Lady Maria. It was, to say the least, awkward. The occasion was an evening party of Lady Ratchett's (it had been her son who had graced my debut ball).

We were invited for dinner, and Aunt Hester assured me that Lady Ratchett's food was always impeccable, and the company above reproach. I was young enough that a good dinner was still an exciting event in my life, and as we waited to go in to the meal, Aunt Hester left me to exchange a few words with another matron of her acquaintance. I was chatting amiably with Miss Smyth, a gentlewoman around seven or eight years my senior, when she caught sight of Clara's mother.

"I must introduce you to Lady Battersley," my friend exclaimed. "Such an elegant creature; I always admire her style."

"I know her already," I said faintly, but Miss Smyth had put out a hand to detain Lady Maria before I could prevent her.

"Lady Maria, may I introduce Miss Coleridge?"

I received the coldest, smallest, inclination of Lady Maria's head. "We have met," she said shortly. Clearly she feared that someone might recall the brief time I had spent with them in London, so she continued, "Serena was a friend of my daughter's—before her marriage."

I did not imagine the slight stress on the word "marriage," or the icy stare; the subtle insults felt worse than if Lady Maria had cut me direct. Miss Smyth felt, even if she could not understand, the chilly nature of our exchange, and glanced quickly from one of us to the other. She clearly had no wish to offend Lady Maria, but at the same time, she did not wish to slight the friendship she had with me. I nodded, smiled, and excused myself; and tried not to tremble with reaction as I walked away. The worst was over now: I had met Clara and Lady Maria face-to-face and survived.

I found myself seated beside Miss Smyth later that evening, when arrangements were being made for impromptu dancing after a meal whose taste had lost its savour thanks to the incident with Lady Maria. Determined that she should not know how much hurt I felt, I forced myself to laugh and make light of the situation she had unwittingly brought about.

"You know how it is," I said as she confessed her embarrassment. "Mothers like to disapprove of any friend that they themselves haven't chosen for their daughters. Clara's father and mine were friends, and Lady Maria was perforce obliged to accept me."

Miss Smyth launched into a recollection of her own childhood when (she said) a friendship with the local squire's son had caused the boy's parents to become outraged.

"Quite innocent, you understand," she added, "but, as they thought, I was 'not quite right' for Tom." She laughed. "When I inherited my late uncle's fortune they thought differently, of course—but the breach was then too great to bridge."

"Did you regret not marrying him?"

"I? Not a jot!" she said robustly. "Tom was—and is still—a good friend. Despite his parents' suspicions, there was nothing deeper between us. Occasionally he comes to town, and we meet and reminisce, but that is all."

Yet you did not marry. I thought the words but did not say them aloud. Miss Smyth and I were friendly enough, but still little more than acquaintances. She accepted my explanation of Lady Maria without query; the least I could do was pay her the same courtesy.

"Now that Clara is Lady Routledge, we rarely meet," I offered, my voice calm. "We were once inseparable."

"Surely your friendship continues." The question in Miss Smyth's statement was unmistakable. "No doubt you will find each other again on her visits to Winterton."

I wanted to be free of the conversation now; thoughts of whether or not my passion with Clara would ever be rekindled seemed folly to indulge. "Perhaps," I allowed, and quickly rose to my feet. "But I think I am supposed to be dancing—excuse me, please."

* * *

In fact, the meeting with Lady Maria turned out to be a blessing rather than a disaster. Over the next weeks, I shared a few more confidences with Miss Smyth; we grew close more quickly than might otherwise have been the case. At balls, especially when all the most obvious of the fortune-hunting Lords importuned her to dance, our eyes would meet and we would swap a knowing smile. Miss Smyth, once deemed not good enough for a county squire, was now greatly sought after by some of the most famous families in the country.

"Ironic, isn't it?" she laughed as we sat quietly after a long evening's dancing at Almack's, in an alcove which, amazingly, we had to ourselves. "I'm sure my head should be turned by this attention, were it not that I know perfectly well what they say when I'm out of sight."

"What?" I asked curiously.

Her sparkling eyes met mine.

"Can't you guess?" She mimicked the deep tones of Lord Malcolm, one of her more assiduous admirers. "'Well yes, she's a bit long in the tooth, but the family is reasonable enough—and she has *money*!'" Miss Smyth caught the baronet's voice with wicked accuracy, and I couldn't prevent a giggle.

"Really, Kate!" I protested, for we were now on first-name terms.

She shook her head.

"Quite true, my dear. I told you they said it when I was out of sight—not out of earshot." She looked at her feet and sniffed dramatically. "As you can imagine, I was utterly cast down!"

But there was a mischievous expression on her face and I now knew her too well to be taken in. I straightened my own face and looked serious.

"I am amazed you felt able to show yourself in public again," I agreed.

She squeezed my hand.

"Oh Serena, where have you been for so long? I can't tell you how much more entertaining these past few years would have been if I'd only met you earlier! I've enjoyed the balls and the attention, however easily bought—but I have missed someone to laugh with. The seriousness of most of the debutantes is terrifying!"

I felt a strange curl in my stomach at the contact of her fingers with mine. For a moment, it was as if we were the only two in the room; the noise of the music and people faded to nothing, and Kate's gentle touch was all I knew. I fought a peculiar impulse to lay my head on her shoulder and cry out my secrets, to tell her everything and trust that she, unlike everyone else, would understand—that her friendship was strong enough to bear the awful truth about my past. But it was a public ball, and besides...I knew that I could tell no one about my past. Kate was the first true female friend I had made in London, and the thought of losing her was almost unbearable.

* * *

After a while, I came to the surprising realisation that I was enjoying my London Season. After losing Clara, I had believed that I would never take pleasure in anything again. When my parents first proposed that I might have my season after all, I was reluctant to come to London. But I felt that I owed it to them not only to go, but to do so with good grace. They had fought for understanding, but I suspect in their heart of hearts they still felt that I had let them down; that I was deviant, disgusting, perverted—the sort of person who would assault a so-called friend in her own house. That they managed to push that to the backs of their minds and to give me their love was something for which I would never cease to be grateful. And if it made them happy to see me a debutante on the grand stage, then I would do so for their sakes. But that I actually enjoyed myself…that was something I had not expected. Granted I had taken pleasure in the sights and events of London on my previous visits, but the circumstances had been so very different then. At my presentation, I had been looking forward to an exciting season; during the brief weeks as the Battersleys' guest, my mind had been more filled with the joy of being with Clara again than with the specifics of the social occasions. This time, older and sadder, I had nothing but the season itself to tempt me to enjoyment—and to my surprise, I had succumbed to that temptation.

I was not a startling success as a debutante. I had neither the extroversion nor the beauty of Clara, nor could I offer the temptation of fortune that Kate possessed. But I was not despised either. My card was often full at balls, and whilst I suspected that part of this was due to my friendship with rich Miss Smyth (as I heard her called more than once in my hearing), it was not everything. Mr. Feverley, bless him, had never forgotten the encouragement I gave him when we first danced, and I truly believe he would have risked his aunt's wrath and spoken to me even if I had been rejected by the rest of the *ton* altogether. He might be shy, but he was intensely loyal, and to my delight, I found that once she got to know him, Kate liked him as much as I.

"I never thought that you would appreciate his company so much," I said to her in one *tête-à-tête* we shared, as we sat alone in Aunt Hester's drawing room. "Mr. Feverley, I mean."

She raised an eyebrow. "Did you think me so high in the instep that I would turn him down?"

I was beginning to have my friend's measure and I knew she was joking with me. "Well, he is extremely different to the usual run of your suitors," I pointed out.

She laughed. "A palpable hit, Serena. He is indeed—and I like him the better for it. You do not know how refreshing it is to converse with a gentleman who is not merely interested in the size of my fortune."

"You think he is not?" I returned, unable to resist a little teasing.

"Oh, his mother is, of course," Kate replied, unruffled. "Indeed, I dare say she knows to the penny the extent of my treasury—which is more than I do, I am ashamed to admit! But Feverley? No, my dear Serena, I most certainly acquit him of having designs on my wealth."

So with Kate and Feverley on my side, and Aunt Hester as my hostess, I relaxed into the frivolities and fashions of the social world. No one could dislike Aunt Hester, and I was grateful to reside with her; in return, she delighted in having me stay, she admitted. Her satisfaction was so clearly genuine. She was an easygoing but practical chaperone. She never refused any reasonable request I made, but she knew enough about the polite world to make sure that I never went beyond the bounds of acceptable behaviour. She took pleasure in arranging her social life in a way that would suit a young lady. Indeed, some of the gatherings we attended were ones that in any other circumstances, I was sure, she would have avoided like the plague itself. Nonetheless, on such uncomfortable occasions she smiled benignly upon us all, and made certain the plainest, poorest or shyest girl's happiness as my own. I admired my aunt greatly for this skill—and, indeed, for not only having the courage to ignore the social hierarchy in favour of a more humane approach, but for managing to do so and yet still be regarded as one of the most important ladies in society. Although they chose extremely different modes of life, it seemed to me that there was really very much less disparity in character between my mother and her sister than one would at first have thought. The same principle of concern for everyone, regardless of station, was central to both ladies' philosophy.

I missed Anna, nevertheless. She was, it seemed, increasing, and had bowed to her husband's wish that she should deliver her firstborn at the country home where he himself was born. It was hard to imagine what Anna might find to do in a country house. Like Aunt Hester she seemed so suited to the fashionable life in London, but when I remarked on this to my aunt on one of our few quiet evenings in, she smiled at me.

"In the future, of course, Anna and Charles will spend the season in town, but this first time—she is due in two months, you know—Anna was happy to retire. And besides, there is a great difference between being forced to spend time in the country against your wishes, and doing so when you are accompanied by the man you love. Anna will be—indeed, she is—very happy. You need not worry about her. When you find a man you love, you will understand." She paused, inwardly debating whether to continue. "I don't suppose…?" she prompted gently.

"No, Aunt Hester," I replied. "I have met no gentleman for whom I feel the slightest *tendre*."

She sighed. "Never mind, dear. It is early still to be speaking of it."

My aunt's words hit a painful wound. For, like Anna, I *had* found the one person for whom I would give up anything and go anywhere, simply to be with her. But our love was forbidden, and Clara was now another man's wife. Even my sympathetic aunt would be unlikely to console me for that particular loss. Murmuring words of excuse, I fled from the room, and paced up and down in my bedchamber for a full half hour before I could calm my nerves and reschool myself in the behaviour expected of me.

* * *

It was just two days later that I faced another daunting social occasion. I was almost grateful for the conversation I had had with Aunt Hester, for during the time in my room directly afterward, I faced the facts of my love for Clara—despite myself, still undying—and had tried to accept the utter estrangement which was all that was left of what had been. This time of reflection was important, for it was soon after this that Neville, Aunt Hester's butler, announced a most unwelcome guest. Aunt Hester was out visiting an elderly lady of her acquaintance, so I was quite alone that morning.

"Lady Routledge is below, miss," he announced. "Are you available?"

I was tempted to ask Neville to say I was not in. But that would have been cowardly—and pointless. I would have to speak with Clara at some time, and to avoid doing so now would merely prolong my anxiety and pain.

"Tell her to come up," I said, trying to sound unconcerned.

Neville nodded, and the expression of vague disapproval on his face was merely his natural look. I took a deep breath and tried to control my emotions as he escorted the visitor upstairs.

"Lady Routledge, Miss Coleridge." As well as a gloomy visage, Neville had a ponderous speech that could make the most innocent visitor sound ominous, but he did not need his skills with this particular guest. Of all the people I wished to encounter in my aunt's absence, Clara was most certainly the least welcome. I got to my feet, and gave a small curtsey of acknowledgment. Neville closed the door softly behind him, I wondered if he was aware of my distress. Probably he was; there was little Aunt Hester's butler did not know.

The pelisse wrapped around Clara was of the latest mode, and indeed the quality of everything she wore bespoke her new status as a member of the titled aristocracy. She was as beautiful as ever, but as I looked closer I realised that her face was paler than I was used to; her eyes looked almost too large compared to the rest of her features. Marriage, it seemed, had not had the traditional "blooming" effect, and I was ashamed to feel a sense of satisfaction at this.

It hurt to see her. I felt my eyes prick with the threat of tears, and dug my nails hard into my palms with a determination not to let my frustration show. Somewhere underneath the finery, my Clara must still exist, and I wanted to rip the clothes from her and find my friend, my love. Yet at the same time, I could not forgive her. I couldn't forgive the fact that I seemed to have taken all the blame for what had happened between us, or that she had been the belle of the London season when I had been sent, disgraced, back to my parents. Most of all, I could not forgive her for forgetting me so soon—for marrying Lord Routledge without even telling me of her engagement.

"Lady Routledge," I said formally.

"Serena..." She stopped. Then, with a gasp, "Don't shut me out."

I wanted to scream *Like you did to me?* But it seemed that the rules of social occasions were embedded in my soul. I gave a small, civil, smile.

"Pray sit down," I said. She sat, uncomfortably, on the edge of her chair. "I hope you are well?"

She nodded. "And you?"

"Yes."

There was a silence that neither of us seemed to know how to break. It lasted several minutes as we avoided each other's gaze, and I fought desperately—in vain—to think of mundane conversation.

"Why?" I said at last, almost against my will. "Why?" I could not form in words the questions I wanted, needed, to ask. But perhaps I did not need to. She knew as well as I what had happened between us, to us.

She didn't answer directly. Instead: "You must hate me," she said, her voice close to inaudible.

I sighed. I'd wanted to hate her. It would have been so much easier that way. Clara looked at me with pleading eyes.

"I don't hate you," I said with difficulty. Then, bitterness overtook me again. "Does Lady Maria know that you are here?" She shook her head. "Your husband?"

"No, he—" She stopped suddenly, as if she feared to say too much, and for another minute there was silence.

"I congratulated you on your marriage, I believe," I said. I used the word "marriage" as a weapon, and hurled it at Clara like a knife. "I would not like to have been remiss. I gather the wedding was a great social success, though of course I was not present to see it." Each sentence another blade, intended to pierce, intended to hurt.

"Serena, I…" Clara began, her face blotched with pink as if I had actually hit her. But this time it was I who could not let her finish, I who feared what she might say. Would she speak of her love for Lord Routledge, the man who had taken her from me? Or would she betray him, like Judas? A Judas kiss. I had received Clara's kisses and they had meant nothing to her. She betrayed me, and that would not change, no matter what she said of he who took my place.

"I'm sorry," I said, rising to my feet. "I'm sorry. I should not have spoken like that."

"I should not have come."

"No." The monosyllabic word sounded cruel, even to me. I turned away, walked to the window and stared out with eyes that saw nothing of the view beyond, filled as they were with tears that I would not allow her to see. "It's true that I don't hate you," I said quietly, "but I can't…I can't bear…" It hurt to see her. It hurt so much. I still loved her, my dear, beloved, Clara.

"No," said Clara unsteadily. "I understand." I heard her footsteps as she moved toward the door. "I am sorry," she said, and when I turned, she was gone.

CHAPTER TEN

March-April

One rainy Monday, shortly after Clara's visit to Aunt Hester's house, I went, not for the first time, to visit Kate. When I got to the Smyth residence, I was shocked to find Lady Maria exiting the house. I am ashamed to say that I slipped down the steps to the servants' entrance out of view until I felt certain that she had gone. But I was terribly disconcerted to see her there. I had not realised that Kate and she were on such companionable terms, despite Kate's description of her as an "elegant creature" that first time. My knock, therefore, was slightly tentative. The butler let me in, and announced me to the drawing room. Kate got to her feet as I entered.

"Oh, it's you, is it?" she demanded. "I have just spoken with Lady Maria about you."

"Oh?" I said faintly.

"You do know," she said, shaking her head, "that you are a most disreputable character. Beyond redemption, I understand."

"I beg your pardon?"

I was cold with horror, too shocked to control my emotions. I don't know precisely what showed in my face, but Kate was by my side in seconds. "Serena!" she exclaimed. "You surely did not take me seriously? I was only teasing."

I fought off a wave of faintness. Of course, it was inconceivable that Lady Maria would have given Kate any specific details of my perfidy: she could not risk the slightest stain on her daughter's reputation. All the same, the strength of her enmity was evident, that she would go so far as to warn Kate away from me. I knew Lady Maria to be angry; I had not anticipated her being such an implacable enemy.

"Of course," I said now, as I collected myself. "I was just foolish, for a second."

"It was unkind of me to joke," Kate said. "But really, your appearance practically on the coattails of Lady Maria seemed an amusing paradox, given her mission here."

I was both desperate to know what Lady Maria had said, and scared to ask. Instead I changed the subject hastily. "So, what are your plans for this evening's revelry? Will you attend the Salvatori ball tonight?"

"Serena..." Kate began, and for an awful second I feared she would press me further about my confusion, but she showed some compassion for my state and desisted. "Of course. And you? And what about our friend Feverley?"

There was a trace of amusement in her voice as she said Feverley's name: she had at first been sympathetic about his stuttering shyness but now, having made his better acquaintance, she took every opportunity to tease him about his timidity. For his own good, she had assured him, and I knew that he understood that it was kindly meant. Kate could never be deliberately unkind.

"He reminds me of myself," she said now, as she caught my train of thought. "I'm quite fond of him."

I stared at her in disbelief, unable to see the least resemblance between elegant, mature Kate and nervous, blushing Feverley. "What do you mean?"

"Come in properly and sit down," Kate encouraged, "or I shall fear that you will run off before I finish my story."

I pushed the fearful thought of Lady Maria from my mind and concentrated on my friend. I began to relax. I sat, and asked again, "What did you mean?"

"This is your first season, Serena; you know me as I am now. Oh, I know you were in town briefly before, but our paths did not cross, I think. My own debut was almost eight years ago. It…" Kate hesitated for a second. "It was not a success."

"But why? You are such delightful company." These days, the gentlemen flocked around her, drawn no doubt not only by her charms, but also by the robust health of her accounts.

"You're thinking of the money," she accused now.

"Partly," I admitted. "But also the way you seem so at home at all these routs and balls and breakfasts."

"*Now* I do. When I first arrived in town it was a very different matter." Kate bit her lip as she searched for the right words to explain herself. "I was shy, you know," she said.

"Shy?"

She nodded. "Yes. Horribly so. I stayed with my aunt in one of the less fashionable parts of London, and somehow the information of my home circumstances was spread around the *ton*. The gentry looked down on me as having pretensions to better myself. Aunt Kitty—I was named after her—told me to take no notice, but I couldn't help it. All those eyes, all those faces looking at me with such disparagement. I wilted under their examination."

"Kate!" It sounded as if she was talking about a person other than herself. I couldn't see the Kate I knew in her description. "You must have been imagining things."

"Oh, I wasn't," Kate said. She smoothed her dress down absently. "'Rich, but so dreadfully common,' I heard someone say at a ball once. I was mortified."

"How dare they!"

"I was new money, you see. Inherited from my father's father, who made his fortune solely in—whisper it—trade! A sin of the highest order. And I was nervous, overawed by London and the *ton*. I took myself at their valuation, and despised myself."

"But you're not like that now."

Kate's expression lightened; she became once more her gay self. "No, I certainly am not! You're wondering how things changed? Well, there were a couple of reasons." I found myself leaning forward, eager to hear the rest of her story. "After my first season, the pressure lessened slightly. The *ton* found someone newer to criticise; I was left to make my way in comparative peace. And slowly, I even managed to make a few friends and acquaintances. But halfway into my second season, my maternal grandfather died."

"Yes?" I was puzzled. How could a death have affected Kate's confidence in a positive way?

Kate explained further. "My grandfather, Lord Gordon. Now do you understand?" she demanded as I laughed.

"A relative worthy of the highest esteem in the *ton*," I agreed. "But why didn't they know of your relationship earlier?"

"Hmm." Kate pursed her lips. "To say that my grandfather was eccentric is probably the most positive way I can describe him. In his later years, he loathed society of any sort and barricaded himself in his Scottish residence. But in some ways, he still shared the prejudices of the *ton*. Although he had reluctantly agreed to allow my mother to wed Father, he was never pleased with the marriage, and felt that a mere Smyth was no match for his daughter. Mother didn't care. It was a love match, and she continued to love Father her entire life. Often," she added, suddenly serious again, "I'm grateful that she died with him in the carriage accident: life for either of them without the other would have been unthinkable."

I squeezed her hand. Although Kate made little of her orphan status, I imagined that life had been hard for her. If she had entered society under the protection of her mother—Lord Gordon's daughter—her reception would have been so very different.

"But the *ton* realised your connection when he died?" I asked.

"Oh yes," Kate said simply. "It was in the notice, you understand: 'Lord Gordon is succeeded by his son, Adam, and his granddaughter, Kate Smyth.' In my black gloves, it was evident that Lord Gordon's granddaughter and the outrageous upstart were one and the same. Since then, the gentlemen have been falling over themselves for my favours. Can you blame me for not taking them seriously?"

"I'm amazed they aren't embarrassed to do so," I said. My mind raced after these revelations from my friend. "After treating you so badly before."

Kate laughed. "Oh, there's no room for embarrassment when it comes to matters of marriage. Fortune I always had; now, the discovery that my background is not so low-class as once believed makes me extremely desirable. As though," she added, "in my gratefulness for their attentions I would forget their past behaviour!

"That's why I have a fellow feeling for Feverley. He knows that by birth he's considered just about 'good enough' for society and the combination of that with his mother's embarrassing social manoeuvring is enough to make anyone stammer. I've been in a similar position, and even if the rest of society scorns him, I won't let him down." She paused. "The same applies to you, Serena, you know," she said. "I don't know what it is you have done to upset Lady Maria, and I'm not going to ask, but I hope you know that you can rely on my support, no matter what."

I looked down; I felt my eyes prick with tears. I had forgotten my own problems in Kate's story, but now they flooded back. Kate's honesty, and now her loyal declaration, shamed me.

"You wouldn't support me," I whispered painfully. "Not if you knew." My hand went to my hair, and I twisted a lock so hard between my fingers that several strands were torn from my head. "Lady Maria was right to warn you away."

Kate put an arm round me, and I leaned into the comfort of her shoulder, burying my face. Gently, she untangled my fingers and smoothed my hair back into place. She was warm and comforting, and I wanted never to move away from her tender grasp. "I can't think of anything you could tell me, Serena, that would push me away," she reassured me with a steady voice. "But you don't have to say anything. I trust you." She sat up and made me do the same, and changing the subject with brisk efficiency. "Now, what do you think about the rumours about the understanding between Mr. Barton and Miss Hale—or rather, between him and Miss *Emily* Hale, for heaven forbid a gentleman in his fifties should seek to marry anyone as young as twenty-four. I have it on the best authority—his daughter," she added in a stage whisper—"that the banns are to be called for the first time next week. Delightful, is it not?"

Kate and I pursued innocuous gossip for the rest of the hour, even giggling over an acquaintance's poor taste in bonnets. By the time I left, the more serious conversation lay far in the past. Only the least shadow of Lady Maria's ill will stayed in the forefront of my mind.

* * *

As the next few days passed, I found myself revisiting the sweet sadness of my recent conversation with Kate. I felt I did not deserve the warm and thorough support which she had given me, when I had offered so little in return. The only way to ease my conscience was to unburden myself to her. I knew that I risked her rejection—indeed, were she to spread the story further, I risked the disapprobation of the entire *ton*; I risked shaming my family. And yet, I knew that however shocked Kate might be by my confession, she would not betray me to the fashionable world. The worst I had to fear (and it was bad enough) was the removal of her friendship; but it was a friendship currently based on a lie, or perhaps to be kinder, on a bed of secrets. I could not hide the truth any longer.

Nevertheless, it took a lot of determination for me to tell her my secret. It was a few days later, before I managed to force myself to return to Kate's house. When I was shown through I was thankful to find her alone, uncertain my courage would hold out to confess my sins if I were given any chance to delay. I risked so much. She was sitting on the window seat, a book in her hand, and I looked longingly around the room I had grown to love, and wondered whether I would ever come here again.

Then I looked again at Kate, gorgeous in a light green frock of a misleadingly simple style. Her hair was caught up in an elegant twist, but her expression was mischievous, as it so often seemed to be. She dropped the book and stood up as I entered, and came toward me with her hands held out.

"Serena! You are just in time to save me from expiring from sheer boredom."

"Hello Kate. Are you free to talk?"

Kate's mood changed when I spoke, as if she were a barometer aware of a coming storm. She took my hands and led me to the sofa, and sat beside me.

"You've come to tell me," she said quietly.

I nodded.

"I will not betray you."

"You may not forgive me," I mumbled, each word an effort.

Kate took a breath. "Would you like me to tell you?" she asked.

"What?" I stiffened.

Her hand closed hard over mine, as if the strength of her grip would demonstrate the strength of her loyalty.

"When you did not say, it was not for me to pry for information," Kate said. "I think I have known—have, at any rate guessed a part of it—for some little time now. Lady Maria's visit, and your reaction, made me certain." She glanced at me, as if questioning whether she should continue. I felt unable to move, unable even to blink. "I forget the name of Lady Maria's married daughter—Lady something-or-other, I think."

"Routledge." I spoke without thinking.

"And you love her," Kate said, "and her mother cannot forgive."

"Loved. Yes." How on earth had she realised my secret, even before it was told? Was my deviance written so evidently in my demeanour? I tried to draw my hand away from Kate's, but she held firm.

"You were caught, I suppose." She shook her head in an almost maternal fashion. "Never, *never*, get caught, Serena." I wondered whether I had heard Kate's words aright. Was she really suggesting that it was the exposure rather than the sin which she considered worse?

"How little," Kate continued in a conversational tone, "Tom's parents—my country squire—had to fear in me! And how much more they would have feared me had they known!"

"You are…you…" I had not words for what I meant. I believed I was alone in my perversion, that for Clara our loving had been just a practice for the real love of a gentleman, and my continued desire for her proof of my own innate wrongness.

"Love women." Kate's tone was matter-of-fact, compounding my shock. That someone else felt as I did was scandalous enough; that she considered it a commonplace nearly overwhelmed me. "Many women do, you know."

"No." I swallowed. My heart was showing a distinct desire not merely to form a lump in my throat but to force itself thoroughly out of my mouth. "You…you must have realised… about me. You—you are being kind, to make me feel less…" Again I was lost for words. Disgusting. Perverted. Shameful. I could say none of them aloud.

"Am I?" Kate began to smile.

"You must be." My voice wobbled a bit. I wanted so much to believe her that I feared to do so, for I wasn't sure I could bear the pain of finding myself let down again.

"Must I?" she teased. "Serena, you cannot really have thought that you were the only invert in the world!"

But I had. That was precisely what I thought. I looked at Kate again, and my heart beat a little faster. I remembered what it felt like when she had held me to her on our last meeting; the warmth, the sweet feminine scent of her. I felt a tingling in my lips, in my breasts, between my legs.

"So, if I…" I murmured. I leaned in toward her, and pressed my lips against hers, just for a second. Her mouth was soft and giving, and before I could pull away, she had caught me up in her arms.

"If you…" she repeated, her eyes full of amusement and desire.

"Kissed you." My words were just a whisper.

"If you did, Serena, I might just kiss you back."

This time, it was she who made the move, one hand behind my head as she kissed me lengthily and passionately. It was—it was not like kissing Clara, and yet it was. Kate was Kate and Clara was Clara and...and someone was kissing me, and I suddenly realised how much I had longed for the physical touch of another person. Kate drew away, her eyes shining.

"I have been longing to do that for weeks," she declared. "I thought...I felt that you were like me, but I dared not suggest it. I thought you might not have come to terms with the nature of your desires, that you would be incensed at the very idea. Then Lady Maria came, and from the very veiled nature of her accusations I couldn't help but guess what had occurred. And still I could not speak—not while you remained silent. I did not want you to feel as if I pressured you into admission."

"Kate!"

I choked, and found myself crying—great, body-wrenching sobs. After all the pain and shame and hurt, finally there was someone who understood what had happened; who saw it not as a dread secret but as a part of life. I had come prepared—no, expecting—to lose my only close friend, yet instead, by finding inside myself the courage to speak the truth, I had mended something I hadn't known had broken: my sense of self. Although Kate had guessed my secret, I knew she would never have spoken of it unless I confessed. I clung to my friend as I cried out the worst of my hurt, and began at long last the first tentative steps toward healing. She reached up a hand to wipe the tears from my eyes, and I tried to catch my breath.

"My nose is running," I said, inconsequentially. It was easier to focus on trivialities in the moment.

Kate laughed a little. "Silly!"

She produced a handkerchief, and I wiped my eyes and nose, and pulled myself together. Since that first night with my mother, I hadn't broken down. I'd thought I was learning to live with my past, but as I sat with Kate, I realised that I had merely repressed it all; I had shut it into the dark corners of my mind and refused to acknowledge it.

"I'm sorry." My voice was thick, the consequence of my sobbing fit. "I must look a mess."

"You do," Kate said. "Come, we must do something about your hair. I can't, I simply can't allow you to go out in public in such a state. Imagine how my reputation would suffer! Even in my earliest, most painful days, my attire was admitted to be of the first class. That someone should be my friend with hair sticking out like that—no, no, Serena, it cannot be thought of!"

She stood and pulled me to my feet, and ushered me upstairs into her bedchamber. She pressed me to sit on her bed.

"Thank you," I said.

Kate poured some water into a small bowl and dampened a cloth. She wiped my face. It was comforting, and cool on my hot cheek.

"Is that better?" she asked.

"Yes. I'm sorry, Kate. I never expected anyone to understand. I thought…"

"You were alone."

I nodded. "Even Clara…even she disowned me."

"What should she have done?" Kate asked. She patted my face dry with a small towel.

"She never spoke, never wrote. They said I forced her. I didn't, Kate, I didn't! I thought she loved me, yet after—Lady Maria—she just left me alone, never even made an attempt to contact me."

"And it should have been different? Love, true love, and let the world go hang?" Kate began to undo my hair, and piled the hairpins in a small heap on the bed by my side.

I felt a lump in my throat at her lighthearted words, and swallowed hard to clear it. "Something like that. Unfortunately it seems Clara didn't feel the same way." I struggled to keep the bitterness out of my voice, but only partly succeeded.

Kate combed through my hair as if she were my maid. Her fingers stilled as she spoke. "Oh, but you don't know that."

"How can it be otherwise?" My eyes filled with tears once more. I sniffed. "Sorry, it's so silly of me to care. But I—I thought she cared too."

"Yes." Kate stroked my face, smoothing away the tears. "And you've had no one to talk to, Serena, no one has understood. I know, my dear."

"She married the first man who asked!" I turned round to face Kate. "The first! How could she? How could she forget so soon?"

"Do you know she forgot you?" demanded Kate.

"It is fairly evident."

"Moving on is not the same as forgetting." Kate smiled at me. "Was she to stay unwed forever, pining over someone she could never have? Give her this credit: as long as you could be together, she did not betray you. Do you acknowledge that you had no hopes of being together again?"

"Oh yes," I said. "But so quickly, Kate!"

Kate's mouth pursed in a moue. "As well then as later. Would you have felt differently six months after—six years?"

"I...Yes. I would have felt less worthless, less easily replaced."

Kate shook her head. "Not fair, Serena. If she could not have you, it is unfair to begrudge her anyone else." Her voice was more sympathetic than her words; her arm slipped around me and she gave me a quick hug. "Not easy, I know."

"No," I acknowledged. This new way of looking at events came as rather a shock; until Kate's words, I had not considered Clara's actions as anything but the cruellest of betrayals. I had—perhaps I had—wallowed in my misery. With no one else with whom to share my grief, I had seen no point of view but my own. "Kate, it hurts."

"Yes. But what good does it do to hold on to your unhappiness, my dear? Clara—Lady Routledge—is gone. You can either devote your life to mourning, or..." She paused.

"Or what?"

"Or," Kate's eyes twinkled, "you can follow her example."

"Marry?" I asked, shocked.

"Move on," she corrected, and kissed me again.

CHAPTER ELEVEN

April

The kisses we shared that day were not our last.

We were discreet. Kate was old enough and wise enough to know the value of discretion; I had learned that particular lesson all too well. A certain amount of spoken and physical affection was acceptable between women, but with my past history—with the spectre of Lady Maria before me in my mind (in my sight, too often) I dared do nothing that might possibly lead to gossip about my friendship with Kate. Nevertheless, I felt somehow younger, lighter. The burden of my ruined love affair with Clara had been lifted a little, not only by this new relationship but also—perhaps mostly—through my confession. Like the relief that follows a boil lanced, the pain had lessened with my acknowledgment of its existence. Plus, of course, every week I felt more at home in the fashionable whirl of the London season.

And there was Kate, and Kate's kisses. Oh, how wonderful it felt to be kissed, to have that moment when our lips touched and a tingle of lightning flashed through my body! Kate's kisses were not Clara's, and they had a different effect: I found myself less desperate, warmer. I felt my body coming slowly alive as her mouth found mine. She would touch my arm, even when we were in public, and the sensation of her fingertips stayed even after she had moved her hand away. When we held each other, in our few moments of privacy—oh! Kate laughed at me as I trembled in her arms. She knew we could go no further than a few stolen kisses, but we both wanted so much more.

The opportunities for sharing such moments were limited. Neither of us lived alone. Kate had what she laughingly called "a respectable lady" to act as a companion, though it was clear that she was carelessly fond of Miss Rigby and, I suspected, had invited her to live with her to prevent the lady from falling into poverty. I, of course, was a visitor in my aunt's house, where we might at any moment be interrupted by butler or family alike.

I thought of Kate as I lay in my bed, alone.

My aunt continued to be a delightful hostess and companion, and found her greatest joy in encouraging me to enjoy myself. With Anna married and living so far away, Aunt Hester had expected to spend her first season since her daughter's coming out without an eligible young lady to chaperone. Instead, she had me—and I couldn't doubt her pleasure in my company. Our time was filled with not only balls and evenings at Almack's; there were breakfasts, rout parties, visits to the theatre: a veritable feast of dissipation. Indeed, so many nights were spent on entertainment that I sometimes privately longed for an evening at home. It seemed I had more of my mother in me than I realised, though like her sister I still found a good deal to enjoy.

My greatest happiness, however, came from my friendship not only with Kate but also with Feverley; seeing one or other of them at a gathering increased my enjoyment tenfold. What was more, it was clear that Feverley regarded Kate and me as his personal good luck charms. By his association with us, he was able to escape the gimlet eye of his mother. Kate, as an heiress (and, of course, granddaughter of Lord Gordon), and I, the only daughter of a good (and, thankfully, no longer impoverished) family, were precisely the sorts of ladies she was anxious for him to attract. By telling her that he intended to go to certain balls at which we would be present, he persuaded her to allow him out unaccompanied. Although Feverley knew nothing about Kate's and my relationship, however, I felt sure that we were not giving him any false expectations. There was nothing beyond a great companionship between us.

One evening at Almack's, Feverley sidled around the wall and appeared next to us. Now that he had lost his nervousness, he could produce a truly creditable bow, and his stammer was rarely in evidence. Preliminary politeness over, a gleam came into his eye.

"You see I have escaped the Gorgon again," he said. Kate had once described Mrs. Feverley as a Gorgon, and Feverley, delighted, had pounced upon the term, rarely referring to his mother in any other fashion.

"Was it too painful?" Kate asked.

Feverley quirked his lips. "A minor skirmish only. I explained that the 'delightful Miss Smyth' had intimated an intention to be present, and my mother was pacified." He looked at me. "Of course, if I could have told her that Miss Coleridge would also be present, she would veritably have cheered me on my way!" he teased.

Kate put a hand to her breast. "Alas, I am outshone by Serena. You pierce me to the heart, Feverley!"

"Ah, but you see I now have the company of two beautiful ladies. Two are always better than one, you understand."

I could not resist. "Not in marriage, surely? Are not two wives one wife too many?"

Kate and Feverley both laughed.

"If such things were but legal," Kate suggested.

Feverley, his expression comical, responded at once. "S-save me! To be expected to marry well *once* is burden enough. I can only be thankful the law prevents the Gorgon from requiring more of me."

"A hard life indeed," I said, mock-seriously.

"But now," said Kate, as she caught my hand and gave it the smallest of squeezes, "you have a genuine decision to make, Feverley. With which of us will you dance first?"

I stroked my thumb across the back of Kate's hand before letting her go, and quickly saved Feverley from the difficult decision. "Oh, but I am already engaged to Mr. Watson for this dance."

My words were borne out by the appearance of my beau, a somewhat rotund figure of a man whose solidity did not make for the most satisfactory of dancing partners. His bow was stiff, and when we took to the floor I was grateful that the quirks of the country dance did not require that we move in too close proximity to one another, as we might have done in a waltz; I was in grave doubt about Mr. Watson's ability to refrain from standing on my toes. He was keen, however, and not unpleasant company, albeit a little paternalistic. Our discourse, in the moments we had in line, principally consisted of my partner informing me what I ought to think about certain issues of note, to which I contributed smiles and agreement. As I watched Kate and Feverley merrily chat their way up the line and back, I could not but feel she had got the better deal. However, when twenty minutes later she was importuned by Lord Malcolm for the honour of her hand, whilst Mr. Feverley and I sipped a glass of champagne, I felt the honours began to even themselves out. By the time the ball closed, Kate and I agreed our evenings had been more or less equal in these terms.

"For," Kate pointed out, her voice tactfully lowered, "although you had to put up with dancing with the appalling Mr. Benbow"—a gentleman who was accepted everywhere and liked nowhere—"I can't help feeling that the amount of time I was forced to spend with some of the most tedious of my suitors more than makes up for your ordeal." Feverley shook his head at her, and attempted to demonstrate his disapproval at our candour, but Kate disarmed him. "Come, Mr. Feverley, would you truthfully choose to spend more than five minutes with Mr. Coker? Mr. Stuart? Lord Malcolm?"

He ruefully admitted he would not.

Aunt Hester called to me at that moment, and I left Kate teasing Feverley, whilst my aunt chatted comfortably to me about the highs and lows of the evening in far more muted terms.

* * *

One afternoon, I arrived at Kate's house to meet Miss Rigby on her way out. She explained, a little shyly, that she was going to visit—"with Miss Smyth's permission, of course!"—an old friend, and would be absent for some time.

"So I know the poor dear would be glad to have a friend to keep her company," she added. She nodded affably at me as she left.

It took some effort on my part to prevent myself from laughing out loud at Miss Rigby's description of Kate as "poor dear," but I managed to control myself until she was out of sight. I suspect, however, that Kate's butler was somewhat shocked to discover a lady in a paroxysm of laughter at the door. Fortunately, he did not know (nor indeed did I, at that point) about the far more shocking things Kate and I would get up to that afternoon. Kate, who was on the stairs, looked down as the butler allowed me entrance. She ran down.

"Serena! Splendid! But what on earth is the matter with you?" she demanded of me as I tried to squelch my mirth. "Honestly, dear, you will go into hysterics." A sudden gleam came into her eye, and she turned to the butler. "Thank you, Williams. I will take Miss Coleridge to my room until she has recovered herself. Please tell any callers I am not at home."

"Yes, ma'am," he said. His gaze of disapproval lingered on his face.

Kate, however, had no time to spare for the ruffled feathers of her butler; she dragged me upstairs. The butler's expression had, unfortunately, only served to amuse me further, and Kate had not been entirely wrong to suggest I was nearing hysterics. It was one of those moments that the more I realised that I ought not to giggle, the less able was I to stop myself. Kate sat me on the side of her bed, and poured me a glass of water.

"I don't know whether to give this to you to sip, or to throw it in your face, Serena."

I took a deep breath and held my hand out for the glass. I knew Kate well enough to know that she would be perfectly prepared to act out her threat. In a moment or two, I calmed down.

"And what, pray, was that all about?" asked Kate.

I recalled Miss Rigby's serious comment "poor dear" and nearly started off again. Kate, who clearly felt that the situation called for drastic action, kissed me passionately and with a thoroughness which she had never before reached. All tendency to giggle left me. Her kisses sent shivers of sensation that unfurled at the base of my spine.

"Kate," I began.

"Shh," she said as she placed a gentle finger across my lips. "Whatever the cause of your merriment, it seems almost fortuitous, for it gave me every excuse for bringing you to my room." She cast a saucy look at me. "I intend to ravish you, you know," she said. "Williams will not come up after my instructions, and Miss Rigby has gone out on what she leads me to believe is an errand of mercy to an old and sickly friend. You are completely in my power."

The words, as Kate spoke them, were more promise than threat. I felt, for the first time, the soft touch of Kate's hands on my back, her mouth on my cheek. She covered my face with soft kisses like summer rain at midnight, and somehow my arms slipped around her as she pulled me backward across the bed. I nestled in against her; my body fitted with a magical perfection into her curves. For a long time, we kissed, and I revelled in the sensation of being held so tightly against another female form. As well as missing Clara for herself, I realised, I had missed *this*: the warmth, the heat flowing through me as if Kate needed only to kiss me to set me aflame. Any lingering thoughts of appropriate behaviour dimmed with my urgency to touch and taste each and every part of Kate.

"Mmm," she encouraged as my hands traced patterns across her body. "Yes, Serena." She paused to kiss me yet again. "But it would be better still with a few less garments between us, would it not?"

The heat flooded to my face to hear Kate speak so casually of feminine love. With Clara, we had been taken on a tide of desire, barely realising that in the process of loving, we had divested ourselves of our clothes. Since then, I had been made all too aware of the shame, even the loathsomeness, of sharing my body with another woman. Yet Kate made it seem normal, natural, even *right*. She ran one finger down the side of my face.

"A time for actions, not words, you think?" she murmured, nibbling my ear.

I nodded.

Slowly, as if she had all the time in the world, Kate began to undress me. My shoes had already been kicked off; next, she slid my dress from me. She did so with great gentleness, and took evident care to keep the dress uncrumpled. I marvelled at her patience, so different from anything I had experienced before. My petticoat came off next, and then Kate knelt, and undid my garters and rolled down my stockings. She kissed the calves of my legs, and I felt a shiver of warmth. Unlacing me from my stays took some time, especially since Kate took the opportunity to kiss my neck, and run her hands over the stiff material more than once. When I was garbed only in my thin chemise, she paused.

"Beautiful, Serena. You are beautiful."

I felt a lump in my throat. It had been a lifetime since anyone had said such a thing to me. I had spent so long feeling disgusted by myself and my desires; yet here was Kate Smyth, a rich, handsome, *experienced* lady, and she found me beautiful.

"Kate…"

Hesitantly, I got up to pull her close, and fumbled a little with the buttons on her dress, until she put me aside, so that I was left sitting on the side of her bed.

"Allow me," she said. She stood in front of me, and removed her own dress before sensuously wriggling her way out of her petticoats. She lifted one foot into my lap, and teased my legs with her toes as she unrolled her stockings. The other leg was treated in the same fashion. She reached her hands out to me. "I fear I may need a little assistance here," she said, ruefully, as she indicated her tightly laced corset. "Stays are not made for easy *affaires*, you understand."

Again, this casual reference to love and physical affection. But by this time, I longed to get my hands back on her, to touch and tease her as she had done to me. She might say what she pleased; words were irrelevant now. I unlaced her with deliberate slowness, making her wait. Before she could realise what I had in mind, I also divested her of her chemise so that Kate stood naked, shameless in front of me.

"Oh," I breathed.

"You approve?" Kate smiled.

"Yes." I pulled her close against me, feeling every inch of her body as she pushed against the light fabric of my chemise. "Oh Kate, yes."

"Yes," she agreed, and hoisted up my chemise and ran her hands under it and upwards until they cupped my breasts. "You are beautiful, Serena."

"You also."

But this was no time for talking. I gave a tug and we tumbled onto the bed together, and kissed, touched, breathed each other in. Kate had disposed of my chemise by now, and for some minutes—I do not know how long—we were engrossed in each other's bodies; in the feel of flesh against flesh, of warm femininity and passion. Then Kate moved down until her tongue plundered inside my most secret crevices, licking, kissing, nibbling with a tenderness which was almost unbearable. I moaned, and reached out my hands to Kate until she slid up against me once more. Her fingers dived inside me as our mouths fused together again; for the first time I tasted myself on her lips and I found myself kissing and crying and whimpering, all at once. I couldn't bear to lose a single touch that Kate might give me. Then, suddenly in a blaze of white light, I reached my peak, my toes clenched and unclenched as my head fell back, and my eyes flickered shut as the spasms overwhelmed me. Kate held me through it all, so close that I could feel her warm breath against my cheek.

Then it was my turn to pleasure Kate. I had feared, in those moments in which I had imagined this situation, that I would fail her, that my lack of experience would leave her dissatisfied. Somehow, though, in the warm glow of her loving, I could not worry. I ran my hands across her small, high breasts, and smiled as she made a small noise of contentment. I bent my mouth down and suckled her nipples, feeling them peak up inside my mouth. Kate's hands threaded through my hair, and her breathing caught a little, and sped up unevenly.

"Serena," she murmured. "Oh, Serena."

I stroked her gently curved belly and ran my fingers through the curls at the apex of her legs before rubbing my thumb against the little nub I knew lay just beneath.

"Yes, *yes*," encouraged Kate. I felt powerful, feminine, desired.

I moved my mouth up to hers, capturing the little cries she made; my thumb never ceased its motion. Suddenly she was rigid, then pulsing beneath me and I felt tears gather in my eyes.

For a long time afterward, we lay there together, content in each other's arms. As time drew on, however, Kate reluctantly got to her feet, and pulled her chemise back over her head.

"Like all good things," she said regretfully, "this too must come to an end. Serena…" She turned back toward the bed, where I was scrambling my way back into my shift. "Thank you."

"Thank you," I whispered. I allowed her to lace me into my corset before I attended to hers. "I feel…different."

"You look wonderful, dear," she said.

We garbed ourselves thoroughly; Kate brushed out my hair to some semblance of order, and coiled it into a coiffe that would last until I reached my aunt's house, and I left her. Left, but did not forget what had happened that afternoon.

* * *

That night, I dreamed of Clara. The dream was vivid: I smelled her scent, felt her light, teasing touch on my breast, heard her happy laugh of pleasure. I dreamed of Clara and woke aching for her, aching for our friendship which had been the most important thing in my life for so many years. For yes, that was it: Clara knew me all through, in ways that Kate—no matter how much I liked her and enjoyed her company—didn't, and couldn't. Clara had seen me as a willful five-year-old, with a constant "Why?" to my parents' every demand. She had seen me go through my difficult middle years, through my confusion and fright at the changes in my body. They had happened to Clara, too, and we had taken comfort in each other.

As far back as I could remember, visits with Clara were the high point of any week. Living without Clara was, still, unthinkable. I had survived thus far, I got through each day—even found moments of happiness and amusement—but with a void somewhere inside me, a place which only Clara could fill. In days gone by, whenever something amused me, or when I felt sad, I would instinctively turn my head to catch Clara's eye, knowing she would have the same reaction as me. As I roused from my dream, I remembered with painful clarity that she was not at my side. I had loved her as long as I had known her, which was all my life. I could hear her voice in my head, confident and happy, as we played at soldiers: "Don't worry, Serry, I'll protect you." She had defended me from villains both imaginary and real, taken my hand when someone scolded me, and led me into all sorts of madcap adventures—adventures I only enjoyed because Clara was with me.

Without Clara, the Serena I had once been could not exist.

CHAPTER TWELVE

May-June

Clara, Lady Routledge, did not stay married even for a year. The death of Lord Routledge was a surprise to the whole of the *ton*, as it came with no warning—out of nowhere, it seemed. He had a chill, it was said; two days later he was dead. I learned the news at a ball. It was the chief gossip of the evening, sending shockwaves through us all. There was an element of "There, but for the grace of God…" and a dash of true sorrow from the few gentlemen who had counted him amongst their friends. Still, I fear the predominant emotion was interest. The polite world loved a good gossip, and rumour and counter-rumour spread through the ball as the Great Fire of London had done in our city two hundred years previously. Lord Routledge had been drinking, and it was overindulgence rather than a chill which had caused his demise; his widow was devastated, prostrate with grief; no, it had certainly been a chill—it had affected his lungs too badly for the doctor to be able to help. Even dancing came second to gossiping: the Honourable Mrs. Wentworth, whose ball it was, looked as though she wasn't sure to be glad that the event was such a success, or annoyed that all of her plans had to take second place to human nosiness.

It was the conversation on everyone's lips, but one in which I had no desire to take part. Kate, of course, knew this all too well. She had seen my face whiten at the news and set herself the task of keeping me distracted, or at any rate distracting the attention of others away from me. She always attracted a certain level of attention, but tonight she was sparkling, and as I knew from personal experience, Kate in this form was almost irresistible. Anyone who neared us was drawn in by her and had no inclination to waste his attention on a nonentity such as me. The only person on whom this technique did not work was Mr. Feverley, who was as kind and polite to me as ever, whilst looking at Kate with a somewhat troubled mien. I did not realise the cause of his distress at first, but after a while it came to me that he thought that my own moodiness was due to Kate's disregard of me. I felt obliged to reassure him on this point; a few murmured words as we danced together did the trick.

"Miss Smyth seems in spirits tonight," Feverley said to me as we awaited our turn at the top.

"Yes." There was a pause as we danced. "She is doing it for my sake," I confided. as we met up again. Mr. Feverley, poor man, looked totally bewildered. I tried again. "Lady Routledge is an old friend, as you may recall from my debut ball. I trust however, that no one else here will remember the connection."

"Oh." Feverley's face cleared. I did not need to make any excuse for my wish that the crowd would not recall Clara's and my friendship. Feverley would have hated in any circumstances to be the centre of the sort of interest that all known acquaintance of the Routledges were receiving. "That is more like her."

"Kate is always kind," I agreed, and the subject was dropped, however, Feverley was left much relieved.

However, no matter the pains Kate had taken to stop the *ton* from questioning me about Clara, she had no qualms about speaking to me herself.

The next afternoon, as we sat alone in my aunt's drawing room, she raised the subject of Lord Routledge's passing, and the effect it might have on relations between Clara and me.

"For you know," she said, "Lord Routledge's death will make a good deal of difference."

"I don't see why," I said defensively. "The connection is clearly forgotten, by Lady Routledge as much as by anyone else. I see no reason that her husband's demise should change anything—except that it means I am less likely to come face-to-face with her, since her period of mourning should prevent her attending any large gatherings."

"You don't see a difference?" asked Kate, ignoring the majority of my remarks.

"Certainly not."

"You cannot avoid her forever, you know, Serena." Kate looked steadily at me. "And she has just lost her husband. Do you not have any sympathy for her? You ought, at the very least, to write with your condolences."

"I would have sympathy for anyone who had lost a close relation," I said stiffly. "As to the rest of it, we are barely even acquaintances these days, let alone anything more."

"You feel nothing deeper for her?" Kate pressed.

"No!" I swallowed my indignation at the question. "Why should I? The Clara I knew—I thought I knew—has been dead to me some time. What should I care if a lady whom I barely recognise has lost a husband?"

"You say that, but I'm not so sure it is true." Kate reached out and gently pulled my chin toward her so that she could look me in the eyes. "Only those we truly love can hurt us as badly as Clara has you," she said. "Wait!"—as I opened my mouth to protest. "I know what you are thinking: that Lady Maria (whose dress sense, incidentally, I still greatly admire) caused havoc in your life."

My smile was wan. I had indeed been about to mention Lady Maria's name. "But?" I demanded.

"Think about it." Kate met my gaze. "Was it Lady Maria discovering you and Clara in a…shall we say 'compromising' position that destroyed you? Or was it the effect you knew this would have on your parents, the effect it proved to have on Clara? You could, I think, have lived with Lady Maria's enmity had it not rebounded to dishonour those you love. When you first told me your story, it was Clara—not Lady Maria—whom you felt had betrayed you, was it not?"

I had tried so hard to forget my feelings of Clara's betrayal. I had almost convinced myself that I did not care about her one way or another. And now Kate had destroyed my house of cards with a few well-chosen words. Clara was not dead to me; she was alive, and *hurting* me, still. But nevertheless, I took Kate's point.

"Yes." I sighed. "You advise me to write to her, then?"

"I?" Kate's face was lit with a teasing expression. "I never advise, my dear girl. I am just suggesting that you consider the real reason for your unwillingness to communicate with Lady Routledge. For I don't believe, no matter how much you protest, that it is hatred which prevents you."

"In the meantime, I shouldn't blame you?"

She laughed. "Precisely, my dear. But for now, let us forget these troubling issues of the heart. It is time I repaired to my own house to make preparations for this evening's revel-making. I assume you too are attending Lady Stillwell's soiree?" I was indeed. Kate kissed me lightly on the head and then vanished. "Until this evening, then."

Her disappearance gave me a chance to think over her words. Kate was right in what she had said—at any rate in terms of the letter. I *should* write to Clara, if only because the lack of such a letter would cause more comment than any stilted correspondence I might send. Besides, Clara had just lost her husband. It would be callous not to comment at all. No matter how changed Clara was from the girl I once knew, I could not cause her pain so intentionally. Consequently, I sat down at my aunt's writing desk and began to compose my response.

Dear Lady Routledge,

I was sorry to hear of the death of your husband.

I came to a halt, and crossed out the words, for they were not true. Lord Routledge had, I felt, taken Clara from me. The news of his death I am ashamed to say, had more pleased than distressed me. I acknowledged the unfairness of my attitude toward the man, who, after all, had known nothing of the love between Clara and myself. Still, I could not bring myself to send such insincere words to his widow. After a second moment, I put a line through the word "Dear," too. It had been a long time since Clara had been dear to me. Frowning, I tried again.

Lady Routledge,

My thoughts are with you at this time, after the sudden death of your husband.

That, at least, was true. My mind had been in a regular ferment since I read the news of Routledge's sudden demise. I could not quite write about the form my thoughts had taken—anger, satisfaction, pain, confusion—but there was no denying that Clara had been in my mind a good deal over the past few days. What to put next, though? There were so many things I wanted to write, none of which were appropriate or even acceptable in such a letter of condolence. I sighed, and stuck to the bland, meaningless phrases so often used at times like these.

The fact that Lord Routledge did not suffer for long must bring you consolation, although your shock must be the greater. I am sure that I am not alone in sending these good wishes in a difficult time.

Best wishes,

Serena Coleridge

There. It was composed, at least. Now I needed merely to write up a fair copy and instruct one of the servants to drop it round. My aunt, however, would no doubt also be writing; the letters could go together. Safety in numbers, perhaps.

Aunt Hester did indeed write to commiserate with Clara on her loss. "A nice girl, I thought, from what I knew of her, though I know Anna never took to her," she said to me. "Your mother always used to tell me what good friends you two were. Such a shame that…" My aunt was clearly remembering the story she had been told, about Clara's rejection of me after her marriage. "Perhaps now she will have a little more time for old friends," she suggested.

"Perhaps."

In my opinion, nothing was less likely. If Clara had rarely come near me when married, her widowhood—which would no doubt throw her more into the company of her mother once again—would not change matters. But it seemed that Aunt Hester was wiser than I. Until the funeral had taken place, I heard nothing from Clara. And for the first month of her mourning she maintained her silence as became a new widow. However, a month after Lord Routledge's interment—and dressed in the requisite black crepe with a broad hem of at least five inches, which in fact suited her fair beauty admirably—Lady Routledge was announced by Neville. My aunt, with kindliness and impeccable manners combined, stood at once to greet her, and spoke conventional words of sympathy which yet became more than superficial through Aunt Hester's evident sincerity.

"It must have been such a shock, my dear," she said, as she led Clara to a seat.

"It was…very unexpected," Clara agreed colourlessly. The lack of sparkle in my erstwhile friend's voice, and the unusual sallowness of her complexion hinted at a woman almost distraught by her husband's death. But looking more closely at her, it seemed to me that she had gained, rather than lost weight, since I had last seen her.

"Of course," added my aunt, "there is never a good time to lose a loved one. I recall the awful distress I felt at Lord Carlton's death, even though we had known it to be coming for some time beforehand. But widowhood before even a year of marriage seems particularly cruel." If possible, Clara turned a shade whiter, perhaps as she considered the possible future years that would now no longer come. "And in your delicate state," Aunt Hester continued, gently, "it must be a difficult time for you."

Clara was with child, I realised with a shock. That, no doubt, explained the plumpness I had discerned in her. I felt as if I had suffered a blow to my heart, which beat with painful fervour inside me. The thought of Lord Routledge, as I had known him, with his hands all over my ex-lover's body distressed me; she, perhaps, making the small notes of encouragement I knew so well. Of course, they had been husband and wife, but somehow I was not prepared to face the physical proof that the marriage had been consummated—of Clara giving to a man what had once been mine. I felt a small rush of guilt for the many times I had kissed and loved Kate since then. But Clara had rejected me first, I reminded myself. Why should I not have done what I wanted with the remains of my broken life?

"Thank you," Clara murmured.

"I was glad to read that your parents are presently staying with you," Aunt Hester went on, little realising how her every word twisted the knife further in my wound. "One needs family around at such a time, and your brother is a little young to be the support you need. A mother's touch is best. I know Serena has turned to her mother in all sorts of distress, and I hope my Anna would do the same if she needed me."

"They came as soon as they heard," Clara agreed, though she showed little pleasure.

Aunt Hester nodded benignly at her. "I'm sure you have heard enough of an old lady's maundering. I will leave you to have a comfortable coze with Serena, whilst my housekeeper and I have a little chat about the mending bills. I'm so glad to have seen you to give you my condolences, Lady Routledge—so kind of you to visit at such a time."

Clara's response to this was unintelligible. My aunt smiled again and left the room. I wondered whether she had realised that I had said not a word in conversation. I suspected that she had, and—thinking that I needed a little privacy with Clara in order to sort out what she saw as a "little hiccup" between friends—she had generously given me it. So well-meant, and so unwelcome!

"I hope you are well, Serena?" Clara said.

"Oh yes," I said vaguely. "I am sure that I am supposed to ask the same of you; however, my aunt has done it so much better than I ever could."

"She is kind," agreed Clara. She took a breath. "I told my mother I would visit you," she said unexpectedly.

"I..." I hesitated. "Clara, do you think your visit is wise?"

"You said," said Clara, looking me straight in the eye, "—last time, you asked if my mother had been aware of my visit to you. My answer then was no; this time, I intended to have no such barrier between us."

I had almost forgotten that meeting, so long ago had it been—and, if truth be told, so assiduously had I tried to put it from my mind. I remembered now the pale, wan face, whose melancholy expression had not been concealed by the fashionable clothes. I remembered how she had leaned forward and said my name, remembered too how I had interrupted her, and refused to let her finish.

"I'm sorry." The words were dragged from me unwillingly. Whatever Clara was, whatever she had done, she had been a good friend to me for many years. She had come to me, and I had rejected her—for good, or at least understandable, reasons, but nevertheless I had turned her away. Caught up in my own emotions, I had not been able to spare a thought for hers. I thought now, as I looked at her face, that maybe I should have tried harder to understand.

"I asked you then," she said, "not to shut me out. Perhaps at the time it was an unreasonable request. I think it was. I ask you now what you would not allow me to ask you that time. Can we not be friends?"

It was both an unexpected and an expected request. So bluntly phrased, it reminded me of the Clara of old, who had never guarded her tongue when we were together. Given all that had occurred between us, however—the brutality of our separation, Lady Maria's angry, vindictive letter to my parents—I could not help but wonder that she should even bring herself to ask.

"What would your mother think of that?" I asked neutrally.

There was a sudden spark in her eyes. "Let her think what she wishes," Clara said, her voice surprisingly hard and angry. She had never been close to her mother; her emotions had been more akin to fear than anger. Now, however, she sounded as if she veritably loathed Lady Maria.

"She could ruin you—us."

"She wouldn't dare." There was still suppressed fury in Clara's tone. "Destroy her only daughter's reputation? Even if she tried, it would ruin her more thoroughly than you or me. For what kind of mother makes that sort of claim about her own child, especially without evidence of its truth?" Her voice became quieter, as she added, "She has ruined me enough already."

"I see."

"And our friendship?" Clara pressed.

"I…don't know." My emotions were torn in so many different ways that I hardly knew how to form words, let alone give a coherent answer to Clara's plea.

Clara was calm again now, one hand rested gently on her stomach. If I had not realised she was with child before, I surely would have done so in that moment. It was a gesture I had seen so many times in women from all walks of life, from the villagers at Winterton to ladies of high society. It was as if they drew strength from the unborn babe.

"I must congratulate you on the prospective child," I said. A small ache of jealousy flooded through me as I looked at her. I would have liked to be a mother, and I knew I never would be. "And extend my sympathy on your loss."

"I received your letter. It was kind of you to write." She stopped for a second before continuing her previous line of thought.

"Even," she said, "if it was just the friendship of old acquaintances—if I could see you without you turning away, if you would but look at me and smile…"

And after all, that was not so much to ask. Clara would not be attending any more events, thanks to her sudden widowhood; on the rare moments at which we might meet, I surely could manage a greeting. Slowly, I nodded.

"Friends," I said.

"Friends," she said in turn, and her smile, even now, could make my heart turn over.

CHAPTER THIRTEEN

July-December

By mid-July, the season was drawing to an end. Although I was looking forward to seeing my parents again, I cannot honestly say that the thought of being back in Winterton—this time forever, as far as I could see—appealed much. At least in London I had friends, distractions. Most of all, I had Kate. I felt guilty as these thoughts crossed my mind. I remembered how Mama had worried on my first trip to London that a month or so of a life devoted almost entirely to pleasure might ruin me for the simple life of the country. My trip to London had certainly ruined me, even if not in the way she had anticipated. But it was during this season that I had learned to love London for its own sake, rather than simply because Clara was here.

I think Aunt Hester understood some of my mixed feelings, though she did not say anything. It would have been impossible for me to acknowledge my emotions even to her. What dutiful child could say that she did not wish to go home to her family? I was comforted by her wordless sympathy, however, and stunned when one morning, after breakfast, she said, her voice matter-of-fact as always, "I've been wondering, Serena, whether you would like to stay with me again next season. I know your mother only intended you to have the one season. I think," she added, her eyes meeting mine with a glimmer of amusement, "she expected you to like the London bustle as little as she did. But if you were keen…?"

I did not know what to say. I could not claim to be indifferent to the idea, for her words had triggered a soaring excitement in me, but I was not sure that my parents would feel so positive about the suggestion.

"I…I'd love to," I said haltingly. "But I don't know if…"

Aunt Hester smiled. "Your parents have agreed, if it is what you wish."

"They have?" The shock in my voice was perhaps not flattering to my parents, but my aunt had taken me by surprise.

"I would not ask you without their permission," she said. "Serena, if you do not wish to come, I will not press you. It may just be the idea of a silly old woman that you have enjoyed your time here enough to wish to repeat it. Or perhaps I should say the 'hope'—for I have taken great pleasure in having you here. But you do not have to accept. I would not be offended. I grew up with your mother's oft-stated criticisms of the frivolity of London society, you know," she added, her tone affectionate as she spoke of her sister.

"I would like it very much," I assured her. Then, unable to believe what I was hearing, "You mean it? Truly? My parents have agreed?"

"Yes indeed. They love you very much, you know," she said gently, "and they want you to be happy."

"I know I do not deserve such love."

"I think you do. More to the point, *they* think you do, dear. So, you will go and spend the next months with your family, and come back to stay with me after the New Year?"

"Aunt Hester," I said, giving her a hug, "I love you very much and know that you certainly deserve it. I shall love to spend another season with you."

* * *

It was amazing—and perhaps shameful—what a difference the idea of returning to London made to my feelings. Now that I knew I was not returning home for life, I found there were many things about country life to which I was looking forward: long rides on Misty in the heat of the summer months; watching the trees change by the season; later, the warmth of our Christmas celebrations at the coldest time of the year. I even took pleasure in the idea of a period of tranquillity, away from the bustle and noise of the city. And when I saw my parents again, I realized fully how much I had missed them.

"Serena." My mother enfolded me in her arms almost before I had time to descend from the carriage. "Oh, I've missed you, darling. And what a lot you must have to tell us! Yes, I know you wrote, but letters are not the same. Oh Serena, I'm so glad you're home."

"I too. So much, Mama, so very much!" I embraced Mama warmly in return. "And Father?"

"Father," said the gentleman himself, "is here—just waiting for your mother to finish her embrace before I give you mine." Mama let go, and I almost ran to him. He gathered me up, as he had when I was a young girl. "Welcome home," he said softly. "Welcome home."

We went into the house together, all three of us. Mama was so full of queries that I had not a moment to answer a question before she posed the next. My father was quieter, but I could see from his expression that he was glad to have me back. When I thought about what "might have been" and the possibility that I might never have had the chance to see them again…I was humbled by their love. I vowed never to do anything that might distress them. My relationship with Kate, though it had always been private, would not be continued in any physical form whilst I stayed at home. I had asked my parents if Kate might visit and she herself had promised faithfully that she would. For the moment, however, I was just pleased to be home, and to have my parents to myself. Later, visits might occur. Just now, we were all more than content to be a small family.

I had originally feared that, after London with its constant social events, I might feel terribly isolated back in our small village. In fact, however, I took pleasure not only in being with my parents, but also in having time to be alone, time just to "be" without the guilty knowledge of an entire list of engagements I was expected to fulfill. I indulged in long chats with my mother: I told her the minutiae one would never bother to include in a letter, and learned in turn from her the local gossip and events of note.

"You will be glad to know," she said, as she shot a teasing look at me, "that your father has finally sorted out the field dispute between the Lances and Freemans."

I giggled. When she had informed me that I was, after all, to have my season, I had thought the field dispute the subject under discussion. Although my father had intended to sort it out many months ago, the quarrel had dragged on past the time I'd left to go to London. "To whom has it gone?" I asked.

"They have agreed," my mother said solemnly, "to a half share each. The consequent arguments about the relative size of each 'half,' and the richness of the soil, are still ongoing." She smiled. "In truth, I think both families would be lost without the disagreements: it adds a certain piquancy to their lives." Suddenly serious, she added, "You heard that the Freemans lost Germaine, I know." I nodded. That sad piece of information certainly had been told in one of my mother's letters. "There was a struggle over paying the funerary expenses, and I understand the local inn set up a fund. Mr. Lance, I hear, was the largest contributor, although he did his best to keep that information secret."

"That was good of him," I said, touched by the gesture. "It is just like you to know all about it, though!"

She sighed. "We would have paid it ourselves if they had told us, but you know Mr. Freeman's pride. It would not allow him to go cap in hand to the Big House: a whip round in the Black Horse is another matter indeed."

We were happy in our close family party. I think we had not been so much so since my London disgrace. My mother was glad to think I was "getting over" my sinful ideas, and my father did his best not to remember those times at all. If occasionally there was a sad look in his eye as his gaze rested on me, I learned not to comment. He loved me dearly, and I had hurt him dreadfully, but he did not say so nor did he harp on something which he trusted had passed. The three of us kept company and did not wish for any others.

* * *

In fact, it was fully two months and more before we received any guests. But in early October, after an exchange of letters, it was agreed that Kate should come and stay. She arrived on a wet afternoon, shaking her head at the rain and asking, teasingly, whether she was to expect such hospitable weather for the whole of her visit. It was good—no, more than good—to see her again. I found I had misremembered certain things about her. She tilted her head to the left, not the right, when she queried something silly I had said; her eyes were nearer grey than the blue I mistakenly recalled. But she was still Kate. She found amusement in everything, and conversed with my parents as if she'd known them forever. "Which," she said to them that first evening, "I feel as if I do. Serena has told me so much about you."

I took her upstairs and showed her the room she would be using. The look in her eye suggested that she intended to kiss me, but I fended her off as she moved toward me.

"Not here, Kate. I can't." My lips tingled with anticipation, but I stayed firm in my resolve. "I told you in the letters—my parents have…anyway, I can't."

She smiled. "Then we won't, my dear. And now, perhaps, you will give me the grand tour of the house."

It was Kate all over: easy come, easy go. She reacted as if it mattered neither one way nor the other. I was glad she made no difficulties, and paradoxically at the same time hurt that she seemed to care so little.

"Next season…" I said tentatively.

"Oh, next season!" Kate cut me off, cheerfully. "That is a different matter, Serena. But that is some time hence, so whilst I enjoy my rural seclusion, let us not worry about the 'perhaps' and 'maybes' of next season. In the words of the bard himself, 'Lead on, Macduff'!'"

It was on the tip of my tongue to correct the quotation until I caught her expression and realised she knew it as well as I. I shrugged, laughed, and led on.

Kate stayed for three weeks. On a couple of occasions, Feverley rode over from Hamill Place on the outskirts of Canterbury, where he was paying a duty call to his formidable mother. My father was slightly inclined to snub him, Mrs. Feverley's reputation being notorious over a large portion of Kent, but even he had to admit that Mr. Feverley's manners showed nothing of his mother's forceful assertiveness. Indeed, quite the opposite, since the merest hint of disapproval shown by my father was enough to send Feverley back into stammering incoherence. Kate and I took pity on him and took him out to ride. In our absence my father had evidently been spoken to severely by Mama, and he behaved impeccably toward Feverley from then on.

It was strange seeing my two friends in such different circumstances. I had found it difficult, before Kate's visit, to imagine her enjoying the tranquil rural life. In fact, however, she seemed to slip into place as easily here as she had the ballrooms of London. I could not help but comment on her apparent contentment, and she turned on the manners of a great lady in response, flirting with her fan and saying: "It is, you understand, quite *a la mode* to spend a little time ruralising. Not in the season, of course, but when there is no superior pleasure to be found, a lady must entertain herself in the best way she can."

When Kate refused to be serious, it was impossible to move her, but I found it harder than ever to believe that she had been so ill at ease in her first season. She had a happy knack of implying that wherever she happened to be was the precise place that she would have chosen. It made her easy company, but I did sometimes find myself wondering what she *really* thought of this or that.

Feverley—perhaps because he was staying with his mother, or maybe because he remained a little nervous around my father—was far more like the bashful young man I had met at my debut ball. The town manners Kate had schooled him into had vanished as if they had never existed, and even when he was alone with Kate and me, his stammer was still a little in evidence. I felt sorry for him, and wondered yet again how Mrs. Feverley's son could be so very different to herself. Nevertheless, I made a distinct effort to attempt to entertain and encourage him. I was pleased when he visited, but often guiltily relieved when he took his leave. Kate returned to London at the end of October. Feverley stayed until the middle of November, and when he too departed, I contradictorily wished him back.

But I forgot all about Feverley after a chance encounter in the village in early December. Our family always tried to buy as much of our Christmas food and presents from Winterton as possible; supporting local village-folk was important to both my mother and father. On a trip to order our turkey for the main meal, I came unexpectedly face-to-face with Clara and her brother. It should have been obvious to me that, after the death of her husband, the most likely place for Clara to spend her Christmastime was with her parents. It had not even occurred to me as a possibility. When I first returned to Winterton, it had seemed bathed in memories of her, and I had found myself looking for her each time I left the house. But after long months without her, the tentative friendship we had struck up at the end of the previous season seemed like something which had happened in a different lifetime; I had thought little more about it.

More fool I. I think the shock was not so bad for Clara. She had presumably been warned of my corruptive presence, though her cheeks, whipped red from the wind, turned pale at the meeting. It seemed that Horace had been sheltered from much of what had gone on a couple of years earlier. He greeted me with the caution of one who knew me to be in his parents' bad books, but with no suggestion that he knew the reason. From his reaction to our meeting, I suspected he had put the quarrel down to "one of those girl things."

"Hello Serena," he said blithely, then, evidently remembering the strictures against me, added "Um... Yes..." in a rather more tentative tone, glancing furtively at his sister in evident hope of support.

But Clara said nothing. After our reconciliation—of a sort—I had expected her at least to greet me. Instead, I was met by a deathly silence which I felt helpless to break.

"G-good morning, Horace." I had never been shy of Clara's little brother before. It was absurd to start now. But with Clara standing behind him without vouchsafing a word, I hardly knew what to do or say. I could see that the date of her confinement was drawing ever nearer. Even if I took into account the copious layers of clothing she wore, she had clearly put on a good deal of weight since we last met.

"Clara," he said, as he nudged his sister in the ribs with the force only a younger brother would see fit to use.

"Hello," she whispered. I felt her looking at me, but did not dare meet her eye.

"You look well," I offered, almost as one might offer a gift.

But it seemed Clara had shot her bolt with that one word. Horace, now shifting from foot to foot with the awkwardness of the child he still, really, was, clearly decided that enough was enough.

"She is," he said. "Well, must go. Er, goodbye."

And he dragged her past me before anything else could be said.

The little meeting had upset me. Was it the unexpectedness of it? It would be unfair both to Clara and me to say that I had felt "safe" in Winterton. I knew now that Clara wished me no harm and would, indeed, have had a closer friendship with me if I had allowed it. But it had been nice to be free of the tangled, tormented emotions that had beset me in town. Now, with one meeting, they were back.

It was at night that the visions tormented me most. My bed became her marriage bed, and I could feel the hot, wine-fuelled breath of Lord Routledge, his death seeming so much less real than my bitter fantasies. I imagined the baby wriggling inside her, distending her belly as it grew. I went further back, imagining *his* hands on my Clara, touching her intimately. And she? Had she warmed under his touch as she had under mine? Made the same sweet noises of pleasure as he took her?

I saw, in my mind, his large hands fondling Clara's breasts, his mouth firm and demanding against hers. Sometimes she seemed unwilling, her soft curves resisting him as much as they could, her expression sad even as she allowed him to do what he would.

Other times—worse still—she enjoyed his attentions, and she herself was the one to fling herself at Routledge, pressing her lips against his with an eagerness I could recall all too vividly. She would run possessive hands down his body as she had down mine, pull him closer and closer into her arms. Sometimes she spoke, telling him how much she loved his masculinity, his strong male body. Every word was as painful as a nail in my heart.

Although I had intended to keep my thoughts from lingering on Kate, at times like this I had to visualise her. I tried to dream that she was with me, if only to keep the worse demons from infesting my brain. Kate's lean, tall, body; the small breasts which fitted so snugly in my hands, and her pleasure when I took them in my mouth. Her smooth belly, so pale, and unexpectedly ticklish; occasionally she would wriggle and laugh under my touch. The brown curls at the apex of her legs, hiding her secret places. That small hardness, just made for the pressure of a finger or thumb; her sleek wetness where my fingers could dive inside her. I would catalogue her, part by intimate part, until I could almost feel her skin beneath my hands.

But when I slept, I dreamt of Clara.

1817

CHAPTER FOURTEEN

January-March

My parents had not told me of Clara's arrival; they did not tell me when she left, either, in the dark, early, January days. I knew only because I had heard the murmurings in the village of "my lady," and listened until I learned that she had hastened back to the smart London doctor who was to attend her in her confinement. I kept my eyes out for the newspaper, knowing that there must be news as soon as the event had taken place. I forced myself not to think about the horror tales I had heard about the pain and dangers linked to bringing a new life into the world. Clara was healthy enough, I told myself again and again: she would come through this. She had the best care available; she would be fine. Nevertheless, I looked forward anxiously to reading of her good health—and with interest as to the sex of the new baby.

It would make a great difference to Lady Routledge's life. If the child was a boy, she would be important as the Dowager Lady Routledge, her place at Routledge House confirmed if not for life then certainly until her son was full-grown. If, however, Clara birthed a daughter, the house would be required for the new Lord Routledge; Clara would be looking for accommodation suitable for a widow and her daughter, possibly in the Dower House on Lord Routledge's estate, or perhaps a smaller lodging in London. A son would set her up for life, but a daughter would make her position—particularly given the circumstances of Routledge's death—precarious.

* * *

Clara birthed a girl. I struggled with myself not to feel glad. A female child would bring difficulties to Clara's life that a male would not, but somehow a girl seemed less Lord Routledge's child, more Clara's own. I would not say that I was jealous, precisely, but whilst a boy might be a younger Routledge, I imagined Clara's girl—Rosalind Selina, she called her—to be a smaller version of my oldest friend.

When I left for London, in mid-February, Clara was, of course, still in seclusion. I was relieved, in a way; I still did not know how to reconcile my feelings about her with my agreement, late last season, to be a friend to her. I was very willing to let the future decide itself. It was more of a wrench to leave my parents again than I had anticipated, though it was no wrench at all to leave Winterton. Winterton without Clara had rarely brought anything but sadness. Even when I had tried to lay the old ghosts aside by riding with Kate and Feverley, I still felt the memories tagging unhappily in my wake. And that awful time, when I'd known that Clara was residing just across the village in her old home, when I remembered that only four months earlier she had asked me for my friendship, yet I could not go and see her as I had done times out of mind…that had not served to make Winterton feel like home to me.

Aunt Hester's delight in seeing me, however, raised my spirits. Anna, her baby now nine months old—a roly-poly smiling boy who won my heart the moment I saw him—had timed her visit to her mother to coincide with my return. She was, despite marriage, despite the baby, the same Anna of old. She bubbled over with vicarious plans for my amusement which she and my aunt had formed together.

"I shall be around for a while," Anna told me cheerfully. "I have told Charles that having missed all of last season, I intend with or without his permission to see a little of this one."

"Yes," said Aunt Hester, trying to keep her face serious, "and you were so unwilling last year to stay away, were you not, Anna?"

Anna laughed. "You know I was not! And how," she bent down and cooed at baby Charlie, "could I complain when the result was someone as darling as my boy?" (Aunt Hester looked at me, "I told you so" written on her face.) "Anyway," Anna said, "Charles is opening our house at least until May. After which"—her expression was mischievous—"I may well find myself retiring to the country once more!"

I saw that this was news to my aunt as much as to me. Aunt Hester could do nothing but gape at her daughter for a moment. "You mean…?"

"Yes, Mama," said Anna demurely. "Charlie will have a sibling before the year is out."

For once I was first with a response. "Oh, Anna! Congratulations!"

Anna's serenely content face confirmed the notion this increase was extremely welcome to her. And, as I considered the matter, I could see that Anna, like her mother, delighted in having young people around her. Her children would be loved beyond belief. Despite the current fashion for leaving children with nurses—or, if they were that bit older, with governesses—for much of the time, I knew that Anna would spend as much time with her children as she could manage—they would adore her as my aunt's children (and, indeed, I) loved Aunt Hester. Girls like my cousin were born to be mothers, and any child they had would be richly blessed indeed.

Aunt Hester was too busy taking in the idea of herself as a twice-made grandmother to be able to respond at first. The light in her eyes, though, showed that she was almost as delighted as Anna herself. "Darling," she said, enfolding Anna in her arms with delight, "darling. That is such wonderful news. The boys will grow up together as playfellows, as, alas, your brothers did not."

In the previous season I had come to realise that the seven years which separated Aunt Hester's two sons was a source of minor regret. In my own opinion, I felt that Frederick and Edward would never have been the greatest of friends. Frederick's interests lay in the gaming table and fashionable world, Edward's in pure mathematics and academia.

Anna smiled. "She might be a girl," she teased. Then, more seriously, she turned to me. "If she is, Serena," she said, "I would like you to stand godmother to her. Would you do that?"

Despite myself, I could not but wonder whether I was fit to be the godmother of any child. Our religion taught that relationships occurred between man and woman in the sight of God: that was what we called marriage. Anything else—particularly something such as a lady's love affair with another lady—was sin…perversion. Anna saw the doubt on my face and drew back.

"If you do not want to…" she said.

I forced myself to look at her. "Anna, if your new child is a girl, and if you still wish it, I would be honoured to count myself her godmother. I only worry that I might prove unworthy of the charge."

She sighed in relief. "How could you think my wishes might change, my silly cousin?" She took my hands. "That is what I wanted you to say, coz. Indeed," she said, in a lighter tone, "boy or girl, I shall count the new arrival as your child of God, so be warned!"

I laughed. "Rather than a warning I should call it a pleasure."

This talk of babies made me think once more of Clara. It had been five weeks since the birth of her daughter; she was still confined to her house. She continued to live in Lord Routledge's London residence, although it was now evident that Lord Routledge's cousin would succeed him. Of course, no suggestion had been made that Clara should move out immediately, though in time she would be looking for her own home. I understood from the London gossip I'd heard that her widow's jointure was handsome enough; she would not want for money. But it would be a new start—another new start—

for her: she had been "daughter" and then "wife"; now she was "mother."

* * *

It was good to see Kate again. We had corresponded through my time at Winterton, but rarely touched on matters of importance. Kate's humorous desultory style made reading her letters enjoyable, yet somehow they were more style over substance and always left me feeling slightly unfulfilled. It would have been unfair of me to have wished for letters of sensual description, since even when she visited I had refused anything but the chastest of gestures from her. Nevertheless, I had felt a lack of any real emotion in her correspondence, and had responded in similar vein. I'd spoken only in passing about subjects dearest to my heart, and wrote more about my day-to-day country life. Consequently, perhaps, I felt a strange sense of shyness as I waited at her door on my return to London.

The butler, I think, had never forgiven or forgotten my hysterics on the doorstep that one time, and looked at me with an air of suspicion, as if I were some sort of performing animal. I smiled at him and asked for Kate, but before he could lead me to her, I saw Kate herself, who swept past the butler and took both my hands in hers as she pulled me into the hall.

"Serena! How wonderful to see you again!" She struck a dramatic pose. "Every second has been an hour, every hour a lifetime in your absence," she teased. She glanced up at the butler. "That is the way we ladies are supposed to express ourselves, is it not, Merrow?"

"I'm sure I could not say, ma'am." His expression was somewhere between outrage and—was it amusement? Kate was, after all, very difficult to resist.

"Well," she said smiling, "buttle off to your business. I will look after Miss Coleridge."

He bowed and left us, and I smiled at Kate. "That poor man."

"Come upstairs." Kate turned toward the stairs, still holding one of my hands. "Honestly, Serena, I have not seen you for nearly four months, and the first words you say refer to the butler! I must be losing my appeal."

Involuntarily, I grasped her hand a little tighter as she led me to her room. "I'm glad to see you again," I said uncertainly.

She closed the door behind us, leaned forward and kissed me on the lips. "I suppose I am allowed to do this now?" she asked lightly. Then she sobered. "Serena, I really am glad to see you, my dear. How are you? You said so little in your letters."

"I'm well." Part of me wanted to spill out everything in my mind: about Anna, about Clara, babies and godmothering, while the other part wanted Kate to hold me, kiss me, make me forget all the confusing emotions in my mind as I concentrated only on my body and hers. "And of course we can kiss. You know it was just..."

"I know." Kate sat on the bed and patted the place beside her. I took the unspoken invitation and sat next to her. "You did not want to desecrate the family home."

"No! Kate—"

"Shh!" she interrupted again, placing a finger across my lips. Then, leaning close, she whispered in my ear, "Desecrate my home instead."

She removed her finger and replaced it with her mouth, in a kiss which was more demanding than I was used to from her. How much I had missed her touch! I moaned softly as I kissed her back with equal passion. My body suddenly inflamed, I needed more—more. We fell back together onto her bed, our hands exploring as our mouths stayed fused. One of Kate's hands was in my hair, tugging it out of its severe style until it fell about me like a dark veil. Her other hand caressed my breast through my all-too-many layers. I slid a leg between hers, careless of our dresses, and pulled her closer, closer.

We had never been like this before, so desperate, so wanton. We had loved, and I had enjoyed the loving, but it had been more warm than passionate. Somehow, though, the time apart had made me want her more; perhaps those nights when I cataloged Kate's body had frustrated me more than I had imagined. Whatever it was, we kissed and touched and kissed again, and rumpling the bedclothes, caring little as the springs of the bed creaked beneath us.

When I undressed her, I stared, scarcely breathing. She was familiar but different. I had forgotten, or misremembered so many things, and I wanted to kiss every familiar-unfamiliar inch of her skin. For once, Kate was prepared to lie back and allow me to pleasure her, and I made the most of her unusual docility to kiss and fondle her all over. She came, suddenly, as I ran my tongue around her nipple, then again as I rubbed the palm of my hand between her legs. And then, it seemed, the old Kate was back. She rolled me over until I lay beneath her, and took control herself.

"Lie still, Serena," Kate murmured, and she slid down until her mouth was at the apex of my legs. I gasped as she placed a row of kisses along the inside of one thigh and then the other. There was something somehow more intimate about Kate's mouth rather than her fingers. The feeling intensified as…

"Oh." The word was drawn out of me unexpectedly.

Kate licked more deeply still, her face half-buried in the curls of my sex as her tongue flicked against that sensitive bud between my legs. My hips bucked and Kate laughed softly and pressed a hand against my belly.

"Lie still," she said again.

"I can't," I protested, and she giggled.

"Would you like me to stop?"

"No." My response was quick.

The sensations Kate caused in me seemed stronger—more intense—than I remembered. Almost it was too much, too intense to bear. She slipped her tongue inside me for a second, then resumed her attention to my swollen bud, and I put an arm across my face, and bit into my own flesh to prevent my screams. I could hear a keening noise and knew that it must be coming from me.

Kate sucked harder, and I cared no more about anything. I cried out as I tipped over into a series of wonderful spasms, aware of nothing but my body and the closeness of Kate. By the time the shivers had stopped, she was beside me, holding me close.

"That was…you…" I had no words for what I had just experienced; occasional shudders still thundered through me like the aftershocks of an earthquake.

"Shh," Kate said quietly.

"I…" I wanted to say that I loved her, but my mouth wouldn't form the semi-lie. I adored Kate, in so many ways and for so many reasons, but I had not the emotion for her that I had once had for another. "I missed you," I said instead.

"And I, you." Kate sat up. "Come, let us dress and be away before Miss Rigsby comes to see where we are."

No sooner had we dressed and gone downstairs, we were joined by Miss Rigsby and the conversation became general. As I left, some little time later, Kate kissed my hand gently.

"Be good," she said, with a strange, almost maternal, tenderness. "Be happy. I will see you soon."

I smiled, nodded, and left.

* * *

It was three weeks later before I saw Clara for the first time, and when I did, I was taken aback. Clara—Lady Routledge, I should have called her—was on the back of a placid chestnut mare, who walked steadily down through the park. Her high-hoofed motion made it obvious that she was well trained and bred. I was stunned. Of all the places I had anticipated seeing Clara, on the back of a horse had not been one. Indeed, I was amazed that it was physically possible, let alone sanctioned by a doctor. I signalled to my driver to stop the chaise, and Clara paused her horse by the side of the carriage.

"Serena."

"Clara!" My surprise overcame my usual reservations. "Are you—is it—should you?…Is it safe?"

Clara had a wistful smile. "I have had to promise to do nothing more than a sedate walk."

She was still dressed in black, mourning Lord Routledge. Her figure was perhaps rounder than it had been before her daughter's conception, though her face looked thinner, paler. I found myself withdraw a little, emotionally, when I thought of Clara's family.

"You are well?" I asked awkwardly.

"Oh, yes." I was not certain whether I imagined the hint of sadness in her voice.

"I must..." I stumbled a little over the words. "...congratulate you on your daughter."

The smile was less wistful now. Clara's demeanour made clear the love she had for her child. "She is a darling. I would"—and it was her turn to hesitate—"like you to meet her, sometime."

The idea brought mixed emotions; I hardly knew whether I wished or did not wish to see little Rosalind. I avoided an answer, instead repeating myself unintentionally.

"And you, you are well?"

"Yes." Clara paused. "Yes, I am—now. And you?"

"I am keeping well."

There was a pause. Just as I was about to motion the driver to move on, Clara spoke again.

"Serena...what you said, at the end of last season...about not denying my acquaintance. Is it...too much to ask?"

Too much? Yes; and not enough. "I would be glad to know you."

"We might put the unpleasantness between us behind us," she offered. "Perhaps share tea, or ride together as we once did."

"We cannot be what we once were. You know that." My heart ached, just a little, as I said this.

"Then let us be something new. Will you ride with me, perhaps, next Tuesday? Certainly that cannot cause us too much consternation."

"That sounds nice." The word "nice" was too limited to describe my thoughts and feelings. Perhaps, however, that was just as well. What else, after all, could I say?

The next Tuesday was cloudy but fine, and I found myself torn between anxiety and anticipation as I waited for my meeting with Clara. Aunt Hester had willingly agreed that I should ride. She had a mare which had once been Anna's, and whose gentle spirit made her an easy, if not exciting, ride. Next to Clara's mount, however, Hetta seemed almost wild. The chestnut upon which Clara rode looked as though he would not shy even were a firecracker let off beneath him.

Clara guessed at my thoughts. "Turgid, is he not?" She patted the chestnut's flank. "But they thought him 'suitable' and I was too keen to ride to argue the point."

"I'm sure he would be suitable for anything," I responded.

"Undeniably safe," Clara agreed, and sighed.

No longer bright and ebullient, Clara was now quiet, withdrawn, changed. Sometimes I found it hard to equate this new woman with the Clara of my girlhood. And then, suddenly slipping through like an unexpected shaft of lightning, I would see her again: the gay, laughing friend I'd known so long. As we walked our horses sedately round the park, we were passed by a smart phaeton, tooled by an elegant lady with whom Clara was slightly acquainted. They exchanged polite nods.

"Do you remember when my first desire was to drive a phaeton with a matching pair?" Clara asked. "It seems like a lifetime ago now."

"I remember," I said, then added teasingly, "but you wouldn't want to be thought 'fast,' now, would you? Although, speaking of fast, sometimes I long for a gallop, as we used to have at home. But that truly would shock the *ton*!"

"Oh, it would put you beyond the pale," Clara agreed.

I glanced at her. The black riding habit was fashionably cut, and suited her well. "We could do it anyway, together," I suggested, only half-joking.

And at my words, for a second she was *my* Clara again: her eyes lit up with that familiar, mischievous glow. "It would be such fun," she said wistfully. "Wouldn't everyone be scandalised? But I suppose I oughtn't—not because I fear the scandal, but..." She sighed. "The doctor has scolded me for riding at all so soon after Rosalind's birth, but I couldn't bear to give up my only pleasure." She caught my eye, and, as always, knew what I was thinking: that had not changed, no matter what else had. "Oh Serry," she said quietly, "your friendship is so much more than just a pleasure."

"Come on," I said. "If we can't gallop, we can at least manage a trot."

Clara nodded. "A trot it is, then."

And so a tentative friendship was formed between Clara and me once again. It had nothing of the emotional (nor, indeed, the physical) intimacy of our earlier years, but still it was something I had never thought could happen—and indeed had never thought that I would wish to happen. Yet it had, and I found I was glad for it.

* * *

It was inevitable that my friendship with Clara must extend and overlap with my friendships with Kate and Feverley. Kate, of course, knew the whole sorry story, chapter and verse; Feverley was tactful enough not to ask. Although it might have been awkward, my lover and my ex-lover meeting in my presence, thanks to Kate, it was no such thing. She extended a blithe and generous friendship to Clara, with a strange touch of gentleness which surprised me. I asked her about it, one afternoon when we were alone in Aunt Hester's drawing room. Kate smiled.

"I always did feel sorry for the child," she said. "I would not have turned her away when she was married and popular. And certainly not now, when some of her erstwhile friends have distanced themselves from her after the rumours."

"Rumours?" I said sharply. "What do you mean?"

Kate threaded her fingers through mine. "My dear Serena, you are such an innocent sometimes," she said, lovingly. "When a lady loses her husband within the first year of marriage, there are always—but always!—rumours. Especially—forgive me—when the lady herself looks so much happier, not to say healthier, than she did whilst wedded. The idea that Lady Routledge was not altogether displeased to lose Lord Routledge is strongly in vogue amongst the *ton*."

"Oh."

"Yes, 'oh.'" Kate shot a glance at me. "I take it they're right?"

"How would I know?" I demanded.

Kate shrugged. "Just a feeling. She's pretty. And, I think, amiable. The two do not always go together."

I looked hard at Kate, but it was ever impossible to persuade her to say anything more than she chose. Instead, she changed the subject, and within minutes we were discussing the matrimonial plans (or lack of them) of the royal Dukes.

Nevertheless, I was aware of Kate's assistance as I tried slowly to rebuild my friendship with Clara. She was quite happy to buttonhole Feverley, demanding that he help her with this or that, whether it be to discuss the latest fashions in the park, or to translate from the Italian some music score. I knew she wanted to give Clara and me time together, without the watchful eyes even of such well-meaning friends as Feverley and herself. We had taken, the four of us, to going to concerts; it was one of the means of entertainment thought acceptable—possibly, given the right pieces of music, even appropriate—for a widow. Kate was intensely musical, so it was no hardship for her. Feverley, as always, was grateful for any excuse to avoid his mother, who was anything but a music lover. And for Clara and me, it was a place to talk, a place to be together. A safe space, somehow, away from our issues and personal distress.

I say that, though on one occasion a concert was anything but an escape. Kate and Feverley had both arrived late, and were seated toward the rear of the audience. Although I had expected them to join us in the interval, they showed no signs of doing so, and I did not seek them out. The first half had been taken up by a requiem. I don't know whether it was this or some other reason which suddenly prompted Clara to speak out.

"I wrote," she said, out of nowhere, as we sat together awaiting the second part of the concert.

"What? To whom?" I asked, confused.

"To you. Afterward."

The "afterward" needed no further description. There was only one moment about which she could be talking. I felt myself stiffen, literally and emotionally.

"I received no letter."

"I know." Clara's voice was low and steady but she could not meet my eyes. She fiddled with the reticule in her lap, turning it over and over. "You must have thought...I can't imagine. My mother tore it up."

"And you didn't write again?" I struggled to keep my tone as calm as hers.

"And I didn't write again," Clara agreed. She turned the reticule over twice in quick succession. "I..." She took a breath. "I wish..."

But her words were cut off by the return of the string quartet. Clara stayed silent throughout the rest of the concert and did not return to the subject again.

I thought about the exchange, though, that night as I lay in bed. Clara had tried to write. She had not, as I'd sometimes thought in anger, jettisoned me as soon as I became problematic in her life. And, after all, I had not written to her. *But that was different*, my hurting soul defended. *Lady Maria would certainly not have allowed her daughter my letter.* My more rational side pointed out that it must have been in the same spirit that she had destroyed Clara's own epistle. Why? Why had Clara not tried again? And if, as she had seemed to imply, she'd still cared, what devil had prompted her to marry Routledge?

* * *

The following morning, Clara and I walked together in the park. I was not sure whether to broach the subject of the letter or not, and Clara herself seemed distracted, so our perambulation was mostly conducted in silence save for comments on the beauty of the spring plants, so carefully tended by the gardeners. The beds were crowded with a veritable riot of colour, shape and size, and it was impossible not to admire them. I favoured a bed filled with a dozen types of blue flowers, each of their own particular shade. Clara and I found a bench close to it, and sat to gaze our fill. The bench was wide and made a comfortable perch. Just beyond us, we were amused to watch the efforts of a young boy to manage his hoop and stick.

"Lady Routledge?" The voice, emanating from behind us, broke into our reverie.

Clara turned immediately and rose to her feet. "Lady Dawlish, good morning!"

I had seen Lady Dawlish before, but had never spoken to her. It seemed that she was an acquaintance of Clara's who had not seen her since the death of Lord Routledge. Her conversation was full of the words of condolence which Clara must have heard so often in the past six months: "such a pity"; "so sudden"; "terrible for you." Lady Dawlish, however, added one more sentence—which most well-wishers had been perhaps too tactful to utter.

"And it was such a good match, too," she said.

"My mother thought so also," Clara agreed.

The words themselves were not unkind, but the way she said them made me turn to her when we had shaken off this voluble sympathiser.

"'My mother thought so'? Clara, what did you mean by that?"

Clara nibbled on her bottom lip, a childhood habit of hers. She knew that she had given away more than she had intended. Not meeting my eye, she said, "My mother was very pleased by Lord Routledge's offer."

I remembered Mr. Freeman's words when he read of the engagement: "*Her Ladyship's been angling for this since the girl was Germaine's age.*" Lady Maria's own pride in her title had always been evident. It was, perhaps, not surprising that she would be glad to see her daughter also a Lady. But I had a strong suspicion that there was more to it than that.

"Clara…" I warned, making clear that I was not convinced by the facile response.

Clara walked on a few paces with me, and diverted her gaze as if to admire the view. "Especially," she added, "in the circumstances. I should, it seems, have been grateful for any offer at all, given my background."

I swallowed, and found that I could not meet my friend's eye. "Did she…compel you to accept?" I asked, with difficulty.

"Oh no. Not compel." Clara's voice was hard. "She merely informed me that I must choose either to be cut off by the family or to marry Routledge. I chose the latter."

I had never really believed in the literal truth of one's jaw dropping with surprise before that moment, but my mouth gaped wide open. "Oh, Clara!"

I reached out instinctively and took her hand. For a second she clung to mine, before reason returned to my brain and I let go. It was the first time I had touched her, even in such a minor way, since our previous intimacy had come to such a shocking end, and I was frightened by the intensity of the feeling this merest touch had brought. I wanted to pull her into my arms and hold her close.

"She said…that?" I asked tentatively. "But—what did your father have to say?"

"Papa? That my mother might, perhaps, say more than she meant, but that he knew I would not be foolish enough to turn down such a respectable offer. In short," Clara continued, "that I should be a good girl, make up for all the trouble I'd put them through, and marry Lord Routledge." We walked a little farther. "I wished I had refused from the very first moment," she said quietly. "If it weren't for Rosalind, I would wish it still…Well, never mind that. But I, I was frightened, Serry, so scared. And my mother—I thought, then, that anything was preferable than to remain under her roof, in her power."

"I understand," I said, and at that moment, I believe I did.

* * *

I told a little of the story to Kate that evening, as we sat together at Almack's, over a glass of lemonade apiece. I kept my voice low, and in the space of two country dances, I had shared as much as I felt able. Kate was a good listener. She had always been interested in Clara, and now that she had been properly introduced to her, her interest had been piqued further.

"So she did not throw you over as easily as you believed," she commented. She twirled her glass thoughtfully between her fingers. "Did I not say that there might be more to the story than you knew?"

"I'm not sure that's precisely what you said," I demurred, trying to remember. But I could remember only how I had bared my soul, and how bewildered I had been by Kate's light-hearted response.

"Next time," Kate said, ignoring me, "take care to listen to your aunt Kate, for she is wise and all-knowing." She stood up and went to meet her partner for the next dance. "You must talk to her some more, though—I'll make sure you do," she called back to me.

It was a few days later that Kate got her chance. She and Clara had been sitting and conversing with my aunt and me for a pleasant hour over tea. Aunt Hester then excused herself on grounds of having promised to visit an elderly acquaintance. Shortly afterward, Kate left too. She made some excuse but I knew what was in her mind by the conspiratorial glance she shot me as she reached the doorway.

She was right, of course: Clara and I did need to talk some more. But somehow, it was hard to start. Instead, we sat unspeaking for a moment or two. Eventually, Clara broke the silence, and it seemed that we had both been thinking of our unfinished conversation.

"I'm sorry, Serena. I must speak of it just this once. I want to—to explain to you."

I clenched my jaw. If our friendship were to bloom once more, I knew we must speak of what had passed between us. But it was hard—more than hard—to speak. Finally, I steeled myself, and forced the words out. "I think perhaps we both need that."

"I didn't write at once," she said, adding hastily, "it wasn't that I didn't wish to, but I thought—I hoped—the time might help. I was not certain how your parents would respond."

"To a letter from the person I had so grievously assaulted?" That had hurt more than anything else: the suggestion that I might in some way have forced my attentions on Clara against her will.

Clara went white. "What did you say?"

"I am merely repeating what your mother told my parents. *She* wrote, you know—immediately. My parents knew—thought they knew—everything by the time I returned to Winterton."

"But..." She looked at me again, as if willing me to recant. "She knew that was not how it was, she knew!"

"Apparently not." I had learned, slowly, ways to conceal my distress. My fingernails bit hard into the skin of my palms, and my toes clenched tightly within my shoes with the remembered pain of that accusation.

"She did know. She..." Clara got to her feet and paced back and forth in front of me. "She told me over and over how wicked I was, and how I had shamed the family with my evil perversion..."

"Shamed *your* family? I was the one accused of forcing you into...forcing you..." I couldn't finish. I blinked my eyes to get rid of the tears that had somehow formed there, and looked away.

Clara sat down again, her eyes troubled.

"I didn't know," she whispered. "I swear I did not." Her reaction was too clearly genuine to be doubted, and it was as if a tiny portion of my heart had suddenly mended. I had always believed Clara knew what her mother had told mine, and she had allowed the cruel lie to stand. Clara went on impetuously, "But your parents believed you, surely? They must have." I swallowed. There was a curious lump in my throat that I could not shift enough to speak. "They trusted your story, didn't they? Serena—" her voice was simultaneously shrill and wobbly, "Serry, tell me."

"I..." The words came out without my volition. "I didn't..." I stopped. The last thing I wished was to parade the idiotic pride which had made me refuse to challenge Lady Maria's accusation. "We did not talk of it."

"You know what my mother said, though," said Clara quickly. "They told you that."

"Yes."

"Serena!" Clara was no fool and she knew me too well.

I raised my eyes to hers. "What would have been the point, Clara?" I asked, fighting a distressing compulsion to cry. "What difference would it have made? I'd lost you anyway."

"The point?" Clara was clearly fighting a similar battle with herself, her blue eyes shiny with tears. "Only your reputation, Serry—only that." She gave a small laugh.

"My reputation would not have been cleared. I would merely have dragged you down with me." I tried to shrug it off, but my voice *would* wobble, just a little.

"I'll tell them!" Urgently, Clara leaned forward toward me. Her hands reached toward me then stopped, hesitant. "*I'll* tell them."

"Clara." I shook my head. "It's past, forgotten. Don't drag it up again. My parents have only just…" I stopped, realising what I'd been about to say.

"Only just what?"

Only just forgiven me. I didn't say the words aloud. "It doesn't matter," I said. I stood up. "Clara, it's over. Let's just forget it. Please?"

"And it is that easy?" she asked quietly.

I looked away from her, and rang the bell to summon Neville. Clara was my past; she could not walk back into my life and take up where she had left off—pre-Lady Maria, pre-marriage, pre-widowhood. The butler arrived, and I turned at last to look at Clara.

"It's that easy," I lied.

CHAPTER FIFTEEN

April

I regretted my words almost as soon as Clara had gone. I hadn't changed my mind about telling my parents, but I knew I had spoken harshly—perhaps cruelly—and that was unfair of me. It was not, after all, Clara's fault that her mother had lied to my parents. That had been Lady Maria's decision alone. I wavered with thoughts of talking it through with Kate, but somehow I felt I could not. My emotions were too raw to cope with Kate's bluntness, even though I knew her advice would be wise. Kate knew, of course, that I was distressed by the conversation with Clara, but for once she kept her comments to herself, and I was left to decide alone. So, after two long days in which I heard nothing from Clara, I finally made up my mind to visit her for the first time.

It perhaps does not sound that difficult, but I was caught up in many turbulent emotions. I would be visiting *his* house, where Lord Routledge had lived. And there was baby Rosalind, too. I had not met her, and was not certain that I wanted to. My Clara, the Clara I had known, was a girl, not the mother of one. I wasn't sure that I was ready to see her in this new light. Nevertheless, I owed Clara this much: she had put much more into rebuilding our friendship than I. It was time that I too found the courage and generosity to build bridges.

The expression on Clara's face when I was announced went to my heart. There was a mixture of disbelief and hope there, which I knew I did not deserve. And then she smiled.

"Serena," she said quietly.

"How are you?" I said, inadequately.

"Well. Very well." She paused a second. "Would you like to see my daughter?" Although she spoke tentatively, there was a touching note of love in Clara's voice as she spoke of her child. *Her child*. How was it possible that Clara was a mother?

"Yes." It would have been unkind to give any other answer, and I confess I found myself more fascinated than I had imagined at the thought of seeing Rosalind. "Please."

"Come with me. She is napping just now." Clara smiled. "She sleeps a lot, it seems." She led me up the stairs to a nursery, where a nurse sat by a crib. Clara nodded to her. "You can leave us, Charity."

Charity curtsied, and left the room, and Clara was by her daughter's side in a second, with me trailing in her wake. Rosalind was a few months old now. Her head was covered in downy blond curls, and she had a beautiful pink glow to her complexion. Her dark eyelashes lay in semicircles on her cheeks, and she pillowed her head with one chubby hand.

"Oh, Clara!" I dared not do more than whisper, fearing to wake the baby. "Clara, she's beautiful!"

"I think so." There was a wistful note in Clara's voice as she leaned over Rosalind, almost eating her up with her eyes. "And so good, too, Serena."

I laughed softly. "No child of yours, then," I teased.

"Far better, of course," Clara agreed. She hesitated, as if debating whether to speak further. Her eyes searched mine for…I did not know what. Unexpectedly, she spoke. "She is named for you. "Selina, the nearest I dared to come to your name. And then…Rosalind." She paused expectantly.

"*As You Like It*," I said immediately. The derivation had struck me the moment that I had read of Rosalind's birth, for the play had always been one of Clara's favourites. I had never guessed that the middle name was there because it resembled my own. But it seemed that Clara had more secrets to come.

"I always thought of myself as Celia," she said, "since her name was so like my own. And you were Rosalind. Do you remember how we used to play that we were cousins? I always had *As You Like It* in my mind. Celia and Rosalind—best friends *and* cousins—I wished so much it was true for us too."

"I never knew."

Clara reached down and stroked Rosalind's hair. The baby made a small noise of contentment in her sleep, as if even in dreamland she knew her mother's loving touch.

"I feared you might think I was silly."

I shook my head, surprised by this revelation. I had always believed myself to be the dreamer, and Clara to be the more pragmatic partner in our friendship. It was I who had the romantic notions, not she.

Clara took a breath, and looked away from me. "Of course," she said quietly, "Celia's family betrayed Rosalind's, too. I did not know, when I named her, how accurate the comparison was."

I bit my lip. "That was not Celia's fault, and it is not yours." The words were hard to say, somehow, but I knew I needed to say them. I looked down again at Rosalind, touched and amazed by this child who had been named for me.

The baby stirred and stretched, opened blue eyes and stared up at us. Clara murmured sweet nothings as she leant down and picked up her daughter. I couldn't keep my gaze away from Rosalind's. It was as if we were exchanging unspoken thoughts.

"Would you like to hold her?" Clara asked.

I had never held a child this young before, but as Rosalind and I continued our private communing I reached out my arms for her. Rosalind was heavier than I had expected. I suppose I had had an idea that she would be like a doll, but she was nothing like. I marvelled at her perfection.

"Hello," I whispered to her. "Hello, Rosalind." I am certain she smiled.

Clara and I swapped no more confidences, taken up so completely as we were with Rosalind, whom I could not help but adore. I had never thought of myself as maternal, but there was a strange feeling inside me as I held the baby close. I knew, too, that confidences or none, this time with Rosalind had brought Clara and me closer than we had been since *before*. Until that moment, I had been cautious, still hurt too deeply by the past to give my trust wholly to her. It had been easier to keep up an easygoing friendship when we met merely at events and I could be, to some extent, chaperoned by Kate (knowing) and Feverley (all unknowing). Rosalind had changed that; and I was fearful, but not entirely surprised when, later, as Clara and I sat downstairs together alone, our conversation once more became serious.

"I don't suppose..." Clara began, then she shook her head. "No, it does not matter."

"What doesn't matter?" I spoke with an effort.

"Can't you...love me?" Clara's smile was weak. "As we once did?" I gasped. I had never expected to hear Clara say those words again. I had never expected to feel so deeply touched by them. I had moved on...I *thought* I had moved on. Clara hurried on, as if to cover my silence. "I know that I have no right to ask, after everything that has happened."

I could not speak. I could not even look at her. It hurt too much. There were too many emotions that I did not want to acknowledge. Finally, I pulled myself together enough for a reply. "I will always care," I said with difficulty. "But..."

"It is the past," Clara finished. "I should not have asked."

I thought of Kate, who had stood my friend—*more* than just my friend—through the difficult season, who had been there to listen, sympathise and advise whenever I needed her. She deserved better after her understanding than to be discarded as soon as Clara snapped her fingers. The aching feeling inside me, had I paid it attention, would have had me fling myself into Clara's arms. But I had done that before, and it had led to disaster. Besides, there was Kate.

"It was the foolish dream of a couple of children," I said, forcing the ache to the back of my conscious mind. "And we are grown up now."

"Grown up," said Clara quietly, "but still foolish, perhaps. I should not have asked, Serena. We will still be friends?"

"I will always be your friend."

* * *

Shortly after this conversation, I became aware of the stirrings in the *ton* of which Kate had told me. A whisper here, a glance there; when Clara and I attended concerts, there always seemed to be someone looking in our direction. It unnerved me, making me fear whether more was being said than Kate had suggested. Thank goodness for Kate, who, when I quizzed her on the matter, promised to do her best to ascertain precisely what was—and what was not—being said. If it wasn't as bad as it might have been—my name, thank heaven, was not involved—it still was not good.

"The suggestion," Kate said delicately, "that the widowed Lady Routledge is not precisely heartbroken by her husband's demise is now particularly strong. Of course, she has their daughter as consolation, but..." Kate trailed off.

"Are they saying she killed him?" I demanded.

Kate laughed. "Oh Serena! This is not a gothic novel! They are saying no such thing, my dear. The gossip merely suggests that the marriage was not a success." She shrugged. "You know what people are. We love to gossip. Lady Routledge's affairs will be forgotten when the next rumour breaks."

"Ye-es," I said, but I was not so sure. Kate had used the phrase "Lady Routledge's affairs" in all innocence, I knew, but the phrase could be construed in more than one way. It seemed unlikely that Clara might have had an affair—but then I had not anticipated her marriage, and as I had spent the better part of the previous season avoiding her, I had no way of telling for certain whether she had indeed been faithful to her husband.

Clara's reaction, when I told her what was being said, was hardly encouraging. The pink faded from her cheeks, and left her face blotchy in yellow and white.

"Clara?" I said, urgently.

Clara smoothed a hand down her already creaseless dress before speaking. "I-it-it wasn't a happy marriage," she said. She looked away from me as she spoke. "He never pretended to love me, nor I him."

"I see," I said, though in truth I did not. Unable to prevent myself, I added, "But why did he offer for you if he did not love you?" And no matter what the pressures, how could Clara ever have accepted?

"I don't know why he offered for me," she said. "Perhaps because I was a debutante, young and biddable, but with a lineage which would not shame him. I do not know. As to my own reasons…" She gave a little laugh, but it had no mirth in it. "I accepted because I am a coward, Serry."

"How could you have done otherwise? You would have been cut off from your family! No one could have expected you to withstand such pressure." I hoped my voice sounded more sincere than I, in all honesty, felt. I, unfortunately, had not been successful in banishing all of my resentment.

"My mother…there was more. I might—I hope, perhaps, I might—have withstood that threat."

"Tell me."

"Later…she said if I did not accept Lord Routledge's offer, she would expose me—us—me for…for…" She could not finish.

"Clara!" I went to her side, knelt by her feet, and reached a hand up to her. "Your own mother, Clara. And so you…"

Clara pushed me away. "Don't, Serry, please. I have to explain…" She took a breath. "You must understand, Serry. Mother could not, of course, have exposed me without implicating you…"

"I know," I said eagerly. "I…"

She cut me off. "No, listen. Serry, I didn't do it for you—for us. You were safe in Winterton, away from the…the…eyes of people. The *ton*. They would have looked at me, avoided me or…or worse. I was scared. And unhappy. And it was…I thought it would be over if I accepted. My mother's threats, my father's disappointment. This was a way I thought I could escape. Believe me, I did not know what my mother had told your parents, though truthfully, I cannot say for certain that I would have acted any differently had I known." She blinked away tears. "He never claimed to love me, you know," she repeated. "I don't think I could have accepted had it been otherwise."

"Oh Clara." I leaned my head against her knee, my thoughts confused. I had felt as if I were the only victim, but that had not been true. At least I had kept my parents' support. "And your father agreed with this marriage?"

"I told you, did I not, that he said he could not imagine that I might turn down such a respectable offer? Later, when I spoke with him again, he congratulated me on my 'undeserved good fortune.' I thought he intended to spur me on to do my duty."

"You thought?"

"We spoke alone, this Christmas, whilst I was in Winterton," Clara said slowly. "My brother Horace mentioned to him that we had seen you in the village. Then, later in the day, Father began to commiserate with me on the great loss of my husband. I don't know what I said, but somehow…I'd believed that he had known everything my mother had said to me, and agreed with her. It *hurt*, Serry, it hurt. I thought I'd lost them both. My father, always previously my champion. I think it was that which I found hardest, that not only Mother, but Father too, had lost any affection for me.

"He tried to protect Mother, to say that she must have 'misunderstood' his feelings, but I knew the truth. He held me like I was a little girl again, held me close, and told me that all he wanted—all he'd ever wanted—was for me to be happy. Oh Serry, I felt loved again. Can you imagine how that felt, after these past years…?"

I could imagine all too well, and I was not sure whether the tears in my eyes were for Clara or for me, for my own damaged-but-patched relationship with my wonderful father. I reached out and took Clara's hand, unable to speak.

"We said no more on the subject, for what would have been the good? But at least now I know." Clara gave me a watery smile. "And now the *ton* is riddled with scandal bearing my name nevertheless. Ironic, is it not? I did not love my husband; he did not wish me to love him. Should I have feigned grief just to keep the gossipmongers at bay?"

I tightened my grip on her hand. I could not allow her to draw away. The anger had died as swiftly as it came, and it was just my Clara sitting there, wan, diminished. I knew I was hearing a truth never spoken to any before, one which she could have told no one but me. Clara was exhausted by the outpouring of emotion. She sat, silent and thoughtful, her demons blinking and weakened after being shown the light for the very first time.

* * *

It was shortly after this that Clara appealed to me once more. She had seen from my reaction that I still cared. Of course I did, I always had. And now that I knew a little more of her history, her struggles, I felt the last of my bitterness begin to fade. The version of events that I had believed—that she had moved on untouched while I was left to bear the burden of our joint misbehaviour—had been turned on its head. My confusion left me vulnerable, unsure of myself, uncertain. It made me, perhaps, act inappropriately.

All I know is that once more, Clara had asked me to become her lover again. It was harder, now, to say no to her. Nevertheless, say it I did.

After all, I had Kate to consider. She did not deserve to be thrown over for a previous love, no matter what the circumstances. Indeed, I flung myself more thoroughly into Kate's arms, and tried to lose my self-doubt and mixed feelings in her kisses and embraces. Kate was always willing to touch me when I needed her to. I was not sure to what extent she understood my mind, but feared it might be more than I wanted. For I knew that Kate knew—or at least guessed—a little about what was going on between Clara and me. On one occasion my two loves met on Aunt Hester's very doorstep. Clara was just leaving as Kate arrived. Kate was, of course, friendly toward Clara, as always, but when we were alone…

"So," Kate said, a little archly, "I was not quite in time to interrupt a *tête-à-tête* between the lovebirds. Perhaps it was fortunate that my dressing took me that little longer than expected."

At Kate's words, I blushed, despite the fact that Clara and I had spent the morning in innocent conversation, talking mostly of little Rosalind.

"I don't know what you mean," I lied.

"Don't you?" Kate's smile was mischievous, but I wondered, perhaps, whether she might be hurt.

"We were discussing Rosalind," I said, my tone almost defensive.

"Of course you were, darling Serena. Of course it is not a case of 'The lady doth protest too much!'" Kate's laugh seemed a little forced. "But anyway, do you attend one ball or two this evening?"

The subject changed, we spent a happy hour together, but later, when I was alone putting the final touches to my corsage I thought of Kate—of Clara—of Kate again. It seemed I always brought pain to those I loved.

* * *

Finally it was I who took the initiative. Kate and I were alone in her room, chatting idly, as she absently arranged and rearranged a vase of pink roses on her dressing table.

Suddenly I felt the words burst from my mouth. "Clara wants me to…to…" Having started, I found I could not finish.

"Be her lover?" Kate suggested.

"Yes." The word came out as a whisper.

"And you?" Kate slipped a pink rose out of the water and through a loop of hair.

"I…"

"I thought this would come," Kate said, her voice matter-of-fact. "It was inevitable. Anyone can see the link between the two of you. I wish you happiness, and…"

"I said no," I interrupted. "Of course I said no!"

"Did you? Why?"

"That's what you think of me?" I stared at Kate, hurt. "That I would simply throw you over the first time Clara beckons?"

"Oh, not the first time," said Kate, smiling faintly.

"It's not a joke!"

Kate hesitated a second, and looked thoughtfully at me. "Serena," she said, "I am very fond of you." I could hear the unspoken "but" in her voice… "Even, I love you—as a friend—and you are a beautiful woman and generous lover."

"But?" I prompted.

Kate pushed a clump of dangling hair back from her face. "It's not true love," she said bluntly. "When we first became… more than friends…you were under the impression that you could not have Clara, that you were separated from her for all eternity. If I could make you—if we could make each other—happy, why should we not do so? But it is different now."

"Why?"

Kate shook her head at me. "You know why. Lord Routledge is dead, and Lady Routledge is prepared to defy her family if she can only have you. And Serena, darling," she added gently, "I've seen the way you look at her, too. The bond you have is soul deep."

"I won't give you up," I said stubbornly.

"You will have to." Kate stood, and walked over to the mantelpiece, absently dusting the ornaments it held. "You will have to," she repeated. She moved the carriage clock an inch or two to the left of where it had begun. "You see, I'm to be married."

I thought I'd misheard her. Kate's words made no sense. I knew she was not in love, and believed that she was not attracted to men in any way.

"I beg your pardon?"

Kate slid the clock back to its original position. "You heard."

"But, but who?" (Also "why?" and "how?" and "when?"—but those questions could wait for now.)

"Feverley," Kate said, in the tone of one stating the obvious.

"Feverley? He's a friend—a good friend, even—but marriage? You're teasing."

Kate moved her nimble fingers on to reposition a candelabra. She turned it this way and that, searching for the perfect angle. "Is it such a surprise?" she asked mildly.

The true and honest answer would have been an unequivocal "yes," but I felt I owed Kate more than that. "You don't love him."

"No," admitted Kate, "but I like him very well, more than any other man of my acquaintance."

"But marriage!"

Apparently satisfied at last with the candelabra, Kate turned to face me. "It's a normal procedure," she pointed out, "and love, I have found, rarely enters into the bond. I like Feverley. I think we will be happy together."

"And he?" I asked slowly. Loath though I was to criticise her, I was not certain that it was fair of Kate to accept a man she did not love.

Kate smiled a little wistfully. "Oh Serena! You live in a world of deep emotions, where love, lust and heartbreak lie side by side. For most of us," she shrugged, "getting through life as best we can is all we ask for. I do not 'love' Feverley. I am not sure that I even know what this abstruse emotion is, and I am quite certain I do not wish to feel it. But I like him and he likes me. Going into a marriage with our eyes wide open gives us, I think, a better chance of happiness than most couples." Her eyes were on me; my jaw had dropped. "He doesn't love me, you know," she said plainly. "We've discussed it and we're agreed that we have something perhaps more precious than this 'love' business: a deep and enduring friendship. Besides which," she added, "by marrying me, Feverley will be finally free of the Gorgon. As if any further reason were needed…!"

"I see." I did not see. I could not imagine entering into such a pragmatic relationship.

"And I want children," Kate said calmly. "I know. One is not supposed to make that statement so bluntly, and you may rest assured I would do so to no other than you. But nevertheless, it is true. I am getting no younger, and my child-bearing years are numbered. I could have married any number of gentlemen in the past, but I did not. I thought for a long time that my desire for a child would be unlikely to come to fruition, for I would not marry for that alone. I would not marry a man I could not esteem, and it seemed improbable to me that I should meet a man I did. But so I have, and Feverley is he."

"Congratulations," I said numbly.

CHAPTER SIXTEEN

April

Although I had only just learned of Kate's betrothal to Feverley, it became evident the following evening that the news was the latest *on dit.* As Kate and I entered Almack's, it was to discover nearly every eye upon us, and when Feverley joined us, the interested gazes did anything but dissipate. The gossips were out in force; certain malicious rumourmongers looked at the gap in age between Kate and Feverley—she was almost a decade his senior—and maintained that she must have entrapped him into the engagement, though even the malcontents were forced to acknowledge that they could not say why she would do such a thing. Kate, after all, was rich, handsome and the granddaughter of Lord Gordon. Feverley's fortune was only moderate, his looks nothing special, and his most well-known relative, his obnoxious mother, liked by almost no one. Counterclaims suggested that Feverley, of all people, was a fortune hunter and Kate an old fool to be taken in by him. I have to admit that such an assumption was marginally credible to those who did not know Feverley well, since Mrs. Feverley had clearly been angling for a match of this nature to occur. Indeed, I believe

Feverley's one biggest embarrassment was that he must appear to have done his mother's bidding.

Lord Malcolm—one of Kate's erstwhile suitors—asked me to dance. His intention, I felt sure, was to question me on this scandalous engagement, for he had never previously honoured me with this request. And sure enough, his first comment—which was, in fact, more of a question—related to the betrothal.

"Never thought she was seriously interested in that upstart," he said, almost as soon as we had taken our places in line.

To his annoyance, however, I played the part of a naïve young girl from the country. "What on earth do you mean, Lord Malcolm?" I asked, opening my eyes as wide as I could.

"Miss Smyth. And young"—he waved a hand in Feverley's direction—"young thingamabob."

"Mr. Feverley? Isn't it lovely?" We broke to dance, then returned to each other. "Such a fairytale," I added for good measure.

Lord Malcolm was evidently half inclined to believe my act, since it was how he had always regarded me, though he seemed suspicious of my apparent lack of details about the betrothal between my two close friends.

"Hmph," he said, and proceeded to ignore me for the rest of the dance, for which I was grateful. The pretence was fun in a way, but exhausting nonetheless.

When he returned me to my seat beside Kate, I could see that she was thoroughly entertained by the curiosity of the *ton*.

"Amusing," she murmured in my ear, "little do they know that this is quite the least shocking relationship in which I have ever been involved."

Absently, I glanced toward Feverley. He stood among a minor throng of well-wishers, accepting, no doubt, their insincere congratulations. Kate read my look correctly.

"Yes," she said, "he knows about us, about my past. In a marriage of friendship, perhaps more than one of love, I think honesty is important. I would not have accepted his offer without telling him the dreadful truth. And he isn't, of course, inclined to the paranoid jealousy such news might bring if he and I were in love."

"Was he shocked?"

"Was he?" Kate put her head to one side, thinking. "Yes, yes, I believe he was at first. His stammer," she said fondly, "came back in full force as he tried to speak about the levels of affection acceptable between ladies, and more strongly still when I revealed that I had gone well beyond anything society might call acceptable."

"He does not despise me—despise us?"

Kate smiled at me. "Have you felt that he does?"

"No." Feverley had stammered a little more than usual of late, but I had put that down to his shyness over his unexpected engagement.

"He is," said Kate, suddenly serious, "perhaps the most decent gentleman I have ever met. When I told him about my past affaires—yes, he was taken aback. But even then, even when I was quite clear about the nature of the relationships, he did not for a second hesitate. I said that I would understand if he wished to withdraw his offer, but instead of shunning me, Feverley immediately thanked me for my honesty. He said (and for the first time I wondered whether this was such a loveless engagement. Kate's expression was unusually soft as she spoke of her betrothed) "that he wished to marry me as I am, not as the world might expect me to be."

"He is a good man," I said.

"Yes." Kate threw off her momentary gravity. "And I am to be the good man's good wife. And now, Serena, I believe you are due to dance with my beloved. Come, let us rescue him from the horrors of polite nothings!"

Some minutes later, I had the chance to speak privately with Feverley. I had, of course, earlier given him the congratulations traditional on the announcement of a betrothal, but he had then been gathered up and harassed in turn by each of the most inveterate gossipmongers of the *ton*. By the time he arrived back near to me, his face was crimson with the unusual—and extremely unwelcome—attention he had received. Kate still remained at the centre of a group of chattering ladies, but Feverley was evidently grateful to sink down beside me in comparative peace.

"I really am happy for you," I said. I think the lack of exaggerated language on my part demonstrated my sincerity more than any overblown phrases. Feverley had heard too much in the way of empty praise than to wish for any more of the same.

He hesitated. "I feared you might be distressed."

"I was…surprised, at least at first," I admitted. "It had not occurred to me even as a possibility. But you and Kate have ever been good friends. It is a sensible match. You will be good for one another."

Feverley gave a laugh. "There you are not in agreement with the rest of society. The compliments of every lady and gentleman I have spoken with this evening have been laced with the strong implication that I will soon regret my forwardness in attaching a lady so much above me by birth and fortune."

"I'm sure that's…" *not true*, I had been going to say, but I caught his eye and could not help but smile, for I myself had heard similar sentiments expressed. "Well, at any rate, it says more about society than about you and Kate. And, indeed"—my smile broadened—"it allows you to take the greatest satisfaction in proving them incorrect."

Feverley breathed out. "You truly do not mind," he said, the relief evident in his voice. "When Miss Smyth—Kate," he corrected himself, "told me of the extent of your…friendship" (and mentally I blessed him for the tactfulness of his phrasing), "I thought you might feel me an interloper, or worse, that I had betrayed my friendship with you."

I felt myself soften. Even when I initially heard about their engagement, it had been Kate rather than Feverley by whom I had felt if not betrayed, then certainly unconsidered. Feverley, after all, could not have been expected to understand the relationship between Kate and myself. His obvious concern about the effect on me when many, perhaps most, gentlemen would have labelled us as disgusting deviants, proved once more what a true gentleman he was. It was, quite simply, impossible to be angry with him. Kate, of course, had already disarmed any reproach from me by pointing out in her gently forthright fashion that we had never claimed to be in love and that in all real emotional terms it was, and had ever been, Clara who was central to my heart. Where that left me now in terms of friendships and relationships I was still not sure, however, the blame for this could certainly not be laid at Feverley's door. Shyly—for I was not used to demonstrative gestures, especially toward men, and I knew that Feverley felt similarly—I placed my hand over his.

"I would never think that. I am grateful for your friendship, more grateful than you will ever know, and I hope that we may continue friends for many long years to come."

"As do I."

I think both Feverley and I needed to exchange those few words for our own peace of mind. I know I ended the conversation thinking even better of my friend, and my heart was more at ease than ever about his and Kate's prospective nuptials.

* * *

Early the following day, Clara came to call. We went through the usual conventions whilst the butler was present, but as soon as he left, her tone changed.

"I heard…about Miss Smyth," she said.

"It was a surprise to me, too."

Clara's hands clenched. When she saw that I had noticed, she relaxed her fingers again. "I thought…" she said, and then wavered. "I thought perhaps that you—you and she…" At that point, she stopped altogether, and looked at me anxiously as if fearing she had offended.

"We were." I could not meet her gaze, and wondered for the first time whether Clara had felt upset—betrayed—by my affair with Kate. Clara had been, if not forced, then certainly coerced into marriage; I, however, had freely chosen to take another lover. And now…now we were both free, and I knew that even now, if Clara asked me again, I would have to turn her down, for my parents' sake, if nothing else.

"I'm so sorry." There was a crease between her eyes. "I did not intend…I hope that this has nothing—I mean…" The unfinished sentences tumbled off her tongue. "My silly words to you the other day," she said at last. "It wasn't…that?"

"You must have noticed," I said obliquely, "the sincere friendship between Kate and Mr. Feverley." It was not an answer, and Clara was too intelligent to be taken in.

"Serry," she said, leaning forward, her hands out in supplication, "tell me I haven't hurt you again. Tell me. Oh, I don't know." She realised her position and drew back, once again upright on the edge of her chair. "You will tell me it is not my business to ask," she said.

And what was I to say? I could not deny that her words had touched me—but if I had not loved Clara, she might have said anything she pleased. And yet, was it that? Kate had not chosen to marry because she felt alienated from me, indeed, I had sworn to stay loyal to her. But almost from the moment I told her Clara's and my story, Kate had been pushing me back gently toward the girl I loved. It was true that the feelings I had for Kate were not the same as those I had for Clara. I loved Kate sincerely, as a dear friend. She was sympathetic, albeit often amused by my worries and fears, and a wonderful lover who took pleasure in my body and had taught me to do the same for her. She would, I knew, have done all in her power to assist me in any trouble.

But she was not Clara, not the girl around whom the world always had and always would revolve for me.

Even my first full season in town had been caught up, in my mind, with thoughts of Clara. For a blinding second, I was stunned by how much Clara had been at the centre of everything I had done. I believed that I had put her to the back of my mind, that she had become nothing to me—but I knew in my heart that the self-deception had been a miserable failure.

Kate had not been so easily misled. She had known and had seen where my true affection lay. Fragments of conversation drifted back to me. On that first occasion, when I bared my soul to her, she had said simply, *"And you love her, and her mother cannot forgive."* Later, when she urged me to write to Clara after Lord Routledge's death: *"Only those we truly love can hurt us as badly as Clara has you.*" Finally, the other day, "*The bond you have is soul deep.*" Yes, Kate knew.

"Serena?" I realised that I had been lost in thought. Clara knelt by my side. "Serena, should I not have spoken?"

"I am sorry." I rubbed a hand across my eyes and came back to the present. "You should not be huddled down there," I said. I gave Clara my hand and pulled her gently to her feet. We were face-to-face, and for a moment I thought Clara would kiss me.

"I am quite well," she said huskily, and turned away from me.

"I am too," I said. "And I am happy—I am delighted for Kate and Feverley. I think that they will be exceptionally happy together."

"I am glad," said Clara, her back still turned.

Abruptly, she brought the conversation back to the safe topic of the most recent three-volume novel, written in anonymous fashion by "A Lady"; although fiction, it clearly referenced certain members of the *ton*. I followed her lead, and although I suspect we were both still very much churned up inside, we did at least bear the appearance of normality, which was perhaps the best for which we could hope.

CHAPTER SEVENTEEN

May

In the days which followed, I realised one thing: Kate had been right when she maintained that the gossip about Clara would stop as soon as there was a new story in town. It was ironic and perhaps appropriate that Kate's own doings had moved the attention of the *ton* from Clara. I had a sneaking suspicion that Kate rather enjoyed the scandal, though she tempered her feelings in acknowledgment that Feverley most certainly did not feel the same way. He had a slightly harried look, and a tendency to disappear around corners when he saw certain of the biggest gossipmongers in town. More and more, I began to believe that he and Kate were a good match.

Clara avoided me. Her neglect hurt me more than I wished to acknowledge, even if I needed respite from the emotions which she brought to the fore. I could not understand why she had given up the notion of our loving one another once more, considering her earlier approach to me. Although I knew that I would have to refuse her, I was yet upset by the fact that she had not asked. Did she really not care as much as she had claimed? Had she realised that her feeling for me was not what it once was? In other circumstances, I would have spoken to Kate about it, but my own reserve on this particular subject, coupled with Kate being taken up with the plans for her wedding, meant that I could not do so. Instead, I kept my anxiety to myself.

But if I felt a little lonely at times, I at least learned to appreciate my aunt and cousin the more. Anna was set to enjoy the last few weeks of her time in London, and she was determined that increasing or not, she should see all of the best occasions. Sometimes, when I attended a concert, I would look across and see Clara staring at me. If I smiled, she would smile in return but would not come over. I told myself it was merely that she and Anna did not enjoy each other's company, but I was bewildered and—I admit it—hurt by her behaviour.

It was, therefore, particularly astonishing when, on the following Wednesday afternoon, Clara was shown in by the butler. Aunt Hester and Anna had gone out, shopping for the little one, they said. I had been invited, but much as I loved little Charlie, and much as I looked forward to being the new baby's godmother, I was struggling with thoughts of babies, of Clara, and little Rosalind. I thought too of Anna, with Charlie and another baby on the way. I even thought of Kate, who had so bluntly said "*I want children.*" And I—I would never hold my own child in my arms.

"Lady Routledge," Neville announced gloomily as he opened the door.

I got to my feet. "Clara?"

"Serena."

Neville closed the door behind him.

There was something different about Clara. A confidence. Her cheeks were flushed and she looked me straight in the eye. "I've done it," she said. "Spoken to him—to my father, I mean. And he says—"

I put a hand out to stop her. "Slow down! What are you talking about? Clara, I've barely seen you in the past two weeks, and now this!"

"I know. I'm sorry," Clara apologized. "Did you hate me for avoiding you, Serry? There was a reason, I promise. I told myself I would not come to you until I'd done it."

"But what has happened?" I asked. "Please, sit down."

Her avidity and excitement suddenly reminded me so much of the girl with whom I had grown up. My heart ached with love and memory.

"I promised myself I wouldn't come to see you until I'd told my father," she repeated.

"Your father? What have you told him?" I felt a strange sense of dread which I could not quite explain.

"About us." Clara looked me straight in the face. "About what my mother threatened. About how I feel about you."

"Are you insane?" Panic overtook me further. I stood and paced the room, unable to keep still. "Clara, what have you done?"

"I have done what I should have done a very long time ago," Clara said softly. "I have told him the truth. That I love you." She came toward me and took both of my hands in hers, and held them so tightly that it was almost painful. She refused to let me walk away. "That I've always loved you. That I can't be happy without you."

"And your father—what did he say?"

"I think it was Rosalind who showed me what I should do," said Clara, obscurely. "Looking into her little face and realising that I would do anything—anything—for her. I knew then, that I needed to trust Father, to trust in his love for me. I knew what I should do before then, but it was Rosalind who helped me find the courage to do so." A tear trickled down the side of her face. She seemed unaware of it, but I stared at it, watching the path it coursed. "I told him everything. He knew that my mother had been angry about us, but he did not know all that she said. He promised me that he would never let her betray me in that way, no matter what."

"And you believe him?"

"Yes." Her response was clear.

I thought of Mr. Battersley as I had known him: quiet, perhaps reserved, but certain in his words and actions. Like my own father, he was a man to lean upon.

"Certainly your father is a man of his word. But you can't mean he approves of what happened between us," I said. "No matter his integrity, your mother—"

Clara cut me off. "What do I care for my mother? Why shouldn't we be together? Serry, after all that's happened, don't we deserve a little happiness? Is it so wrong to hope?" The sparkle in her eye was unmistakeable.

"I can't," I whispered.

"You can…if you will," she urged.

My eyes met hers. "And how do you suggest we conduct our love affair? Am I to take up permanent residence with my aunt in order to be close to you? Your father might have promised to hold Lady Maria back from exposing you as a deviant, but he is hardly likely to encourage you to practice your deviance under his roof. Besides, I could not let down my parents again by—"

"You need not say it." Clara looked away from me. "Heaven knows what your parents must think of me." I did not respond. They thought her an innocent victim of my unnatural passion, and Clara knew that as well as I. "But," she said, "it could be different now."

"How?"

"You could live with me."

I stared at her. "You mean, defy the world? Be careless of the scandal we might cause? Like the Ladies of Llangollen? I couldn't do that to my parents, you know that."

Clara took my hand and led me to the sofa, where we sat together, our knees just a centimetre apart. "Why would the world have to know?" she asked, her voice low. "I am a widow with a child. If I employ a companion, why should they question it?"

"I won't take your money."

Clara sighed, and rubbed her thumb across the back of my hand soothingly. "It would be our money, Serena, dearest. And do you really think that the *ton* would inquire into our financial affairs? We would allow them to make the obvious assumption. Oh Serry, surely you know that I'm not trying to bribe you, darling. Don't you?"

I watched her thumb move on my hand, back and forth, back and forth. I was on the point of tears and could only control myself by making my voice dull, monotonous. "I know that. But..."

"If you're thinking that you would be despised for your dependent position," Clara interrupted me, "you need not. If Miss Smyth—or Mrs. Feverley, as she will be—accepts you, the rest of the polite world would not be far behind. And I'm sure she..."

"She would acknowledge me," I said. "Feverley would too. But..." I bit my lip hard in an effort to keep my distress from her. "I cannot do it, Clara. I can't bring such dishonour to my parents again."

"Think about it." Clara lifted my hand and pressed a kiss to it. It burnt where her lips touched my skin, and I wanted so much to pull her close to me. But I could not. I must not. "That's all I ask, Serry. Just consider it."

I nodded. I knew my view would not change, but I could not bear to send her away with no hope. Perhaps it was crueller of me not to make the final breach then, but with Clara beside me, looking at me as if I were all that mattered in the world—I could not spurn her entirely. She left, and I sat in my aunt's room for a long time.

* * *

Some hours later, as I attended to some letters in the drawing room, the butler brought the news that Kate had arrived.

"Send her in," I said wearily.

Sometimes I thought Kate did not know the meaning of sadness or fatigue. Since her betrothal she had become more indefatigable than ever, and she tripped gaily into the room behind Neville.

"I," she said impressively, "have been shopping. You would be amazed—nay, you would be astounded—at the amount of preparation which takes place around a wedding."

I tried to smile. "I'm sure I would."

Kate fixed her unnervingly direct gaze upon me. "Serena," she said warningly. "What's happened? You don't seem yourself."

"I'm fine. Really," I lied, "I'm quite well."

Kate pursed her lips together as if determined not to say what was in her mind. Instead, she sat down carefully. "I am surprised not to find Clara here. I felt sure that she would call this afternoon."

"She did." I was certain that Kate knew it, as well. I wondered how much she did know—and how much she guessed.

"And?"

"She continues very well," I said, "considering the shocks and changes in her life that have beset her during recent months. She has managed to pull through in great health. And, indeed," I blushed a little at this point, "she looks more beautiful than ever, I believe."

"Hmm."

"So tell me," I said, "what have you bought today?"

Kate ignored this obvious attempt to change the subject. "Has she changed her mind or did you turn her down?" she demanded. "No, don't answer that. I know how Clara feels, that she loves you. It's clear whenever I see you both. And she's told me a little about how she feels." My shock must have been visible. "Yes, I manage to speak to her occasionally, despite your best attempts to keep her to yourself," she added. "She's a nice girl. I always thought she seemed like one. So if it is not she… you must have refused her."

"How could I do anything else?" I asked unhappily.

"How could you do anything but agree?" Kate retorted. "Really, Serena! The love of your life throws herself at your feet—and you turn her down! I despair of you."

"Kate…" I wanted sympathy. I wanted someone to understand that it wasn't that simple—not just a case of love conquering all. "My family—their good name…I might have lost it for them in the past; I must not betray them again."

"So instead you betray yourself. Not to mention Clara."

I stood up shakily and made my way to the door. My heart beat so hard that I was fearful I might faint. At the same time, I felt a wave of sickness overtake me.

"Excuse me," I said, my voice quavering. "I must—"

I could not even finish the sentence, but ran quickly up the stairs to my room. Was I right or wrong? I did not know, but I knew that I had done what I must, however much it hurt. I sat on the floor in my bedchamber, my arms clasped round my legs, and cried.

* * *

Two days later, I ran away from Aunt Hester, from Anna, London, Kate and Feverley, and most of all, from Clara. I cannot honestly describe my return to Winterton in any other fashion. I knew what Clara wanted, what Kate would have encouraged me to do, but I could not do it. Mama had been so understanding, so kind, before. Clara might be prepared to defy her unsympathetic mother; I could not bring myself to hurt my dearly beloved parents, not even for Clara's sake. At the same time, though, I knew I could never marry, feeling as I did. My heart was Clara's. I would give neither body nor soul to any man. I talked to Aunt Hester before I left, and explained that I was terribly homesick for my parents. My aunt, as always, was understanding, although she tried to persuade me to stay, she did not criticise when it became clear that I was not going to change my mind. Indeed, she made it easier for me to leave than I deserved, and I spent my homeward journey in a state of guilt over the way I had treated her.

It was afternoon when I arrived home. The expression I caught on my mother's face when I appeared unannounced almost broke my heart, though it made my resolution all the stronger. I saw at a glance that she feared what might have brought me home so unexpectedly: another scandal, perhaps less easily covered up than the first? Bravely, she fought her anxiety and greeted me with a determined smile.

"Serena, darling."

I was in her arms at once. "I wanted to come home, Mama. I had to come home."

My mother's arms closed tightly around me, and I knew her concern was increased, rather than allayed, by what I had said.

"You're not..." She hesitated. "Not ill?"

I answered both the spoken and unspoken question at once.

"Nothing is wrong, Mama. I promise."

"Then...?"

From within the comforting encirclement of her arms, I twisted so that I could see her face.

"I will not marry," I said baldly.

"You can't know that, Serena." Mother was trying to comfort me. She did not realise that marriage was the least of my concerns.

I tried again. "I do not wish to marry," I told her. "I do not think I ever will."

Mama was silent for a moment. "You are sure?" she asked bravely.

"Yes."

I think, even then, she knew what my words implied. My parents had hoped that my relationship with Clara had been a passing phase, part of my initiation into adult love, a step on the way to understanding what would be expected of me in marriage. Telling my mother that I did not want to share my life with a man under any circumstances robbed her of this hope. And it hurt her, no matter how much she tried not to show it.

"I see." Mama held me close again. "You were right to come home, darling."

That was all that she said, and Father said not a word in criticism or commendation. I had made my decision, and they were kind enough—understanding enough—to allow me that. I had seen too much in London: forced marriages between girls too young to know better and men too old to care; marriages of convenience (one might class Kate's amongst these were it not for my knowledge that she and Feverley enjoyed their association so much); marriages based on a lack of knowledge that were close to being an absolute lie. My parents might not understand my reasons, but they would unfailingly support my decision. And it was for that reason that the idea of doing something—anything—that might hurt them, was unthinkable.

That being said, of course, I longed for my friends. I received letters from both Kate and Clara in my first week at home. Kate's arrived first.

Dear Serena,

You have run away, have you not? Shame upon you for such cowardice! Mr. Feverley—George, as I must learn to call him, though not in public, of course—feared you were distressed by our engagement. I told him this was all too true, and that you had sought solitude to nurse your deeply held passion for him…In punishment for this, I have been ordered—I beg pardon, invited—to a formal dinner with the Gorgon. I can only hope I am intended as a guest and not as the meal. Mr. F. is becoming altogether too good at revenging himself on me.

But never mind that! About you. Clara (I cannot bring myself to describe her as Lady Routledge even on paper, I am afraid: I knew her for so long from your conversation before we ever met. Now, watching her pine for someone unnamed who has disappeared, it seems inappropriate to call her by her husband's name. Goodness! What a digression! Anyway…) Clara is quiet, even for her. She seems to have made precious few friends during her marriage, though the little she says about that time does not make me so very surprised. I am loath to say this of anyone, but it is hard to regret her husband's death.

What Clara really needs is the love of a good woman. Just consider *the possibility, Serena. Love like yours should not be left to wither and die in misery.*

Now, I have finished with the lecture—and, indeed, with the letter, for it seems that prospective brides have all too much to attend to. I'm grateful never to have wed before!

Love, as always, Kate.

Clara's letter was shorter and less exuberant.

Dearest Serena,

I feel as if I have driven you from London. I never intended to do so. Serry, if you wish to return, I promise I will say no more on the subject.

Miss Smyth seems very happy. Her engagement is no longer the latest on dit, *since, because of his debts, Lord Marricot has been forced to go abroad. Miss Smyth would be glad to see you, I know—Mr. Feverley, too. And I, but I promised not to speak of that.*

Love, Clara.

Reading the letters from my friends was surprisingly painful. Every word of Kate's brought her to my mind: vital, laughing, still seeing life as an amusing pageant, yet with the understanding that it was not so for all of us. "*Love likes yours should not be left to wither and die in misery.*" Ever since my return home I had felt—yes, "withered." Without Clara, I would always be somehow diminished. It was difficult, too, to respond to letters like these. Kate, whose parents had died when she was but a girl, could not be expected to understand my feelings of loyalty to my family. Kate's motto had ever been "Do what you want, and don't get caught," but if I were to take up a position as Lady Routledge's alleged companion, my parents would be all too aware of the reality of the situation. The fact that society at large, knowing nothing, would therefore not be shocked was irrelevant. In many ways I could cope with the disapprobation of the polite world *en masse* more easily than my own parents' disappointment. As to Clara herself, if I had had a mother like Lady Maria, I too would have been more than willing to defy her. For Mr. Battersley I felt more sympathy, particularly considering his response to Clara's story, but then, he had allowed Lady Maria to force Clara into an unwanted and deeply unhappy marriage, for which—as I learned more about that brief year—I found it harder and harder to forgive him.

It took a few days before I felt strong enough to respond to my friends' letters. I wrote first to Kate, to whose mixture of censure and lighthearted comment I could more easily reply than to Clara's evident distress. I said nothing about the contents of my correspondence to Mama, and she, with her usual gentle tact, asked no questions. I had told her about Kate's recent betrothal to Feverley. My mother had been interested, especially since she remembered both parties well from the previous October. But I had seen the marks of regret on her face that it was not, and would not be, my own engagement of which I spoke, and thereafter made little reference to the event. I had not, of course, told her of the deeper bond that Kate and I had shared. It would have hurt her for no good reason and taken away the pleasure she gained from listening to my descriptions of Kate in full wedding preparation. And so, when she saw my letter addressed to Miss Smyth, my mother's only comment was that she hoped I had passed on her sincere congratulations and best wishes on the betrothal. I promised I had, but did not venture any further information.

As it was, it took me several drafts to write something which I felt I could send to Kate. Lines were written, crossed out, written in again, words changed or deleted. Even when I directed the letter with her address, I was still unhappy with what I had written.

Kate,

I'm sorry I did not reply earlier—the truth is I knew not what to say. We know each other's arguments so well that I will not bore you with the repetition. I will just say that I miss you all so very deeply.

I am also regretful that I must miss the entertainment of watching you perform all the tasks of prospective marriage. Pray tell me how the evening with Mrs. Feverley transpired. Is she really the Gorgon of our imaginings? I am glad Mr. Feverley knows how to deal with you, and very pleased that he has no intention of becoming a browbeaten husband. Tell him I wish him luck in keeping you in order (something I never succeeded in doing!). My mother sends her congratulations on your engagement.

Look after Clara for me. Well, I know that you will do that anyway; you will be unable to help yourself. At least she is well out of a loveless marriage. I miss you.

Love, Serena.

After the letter had gone I spent a long time wishing it was I, and not the paper, on its way to London. Tell myself as often as I might that I had done the right thing in coming home, I couldn't avoid the stab of regret, particularly at night when I curled up alone in bed with nothing to do save think, and hope to sleep. Having written to Kate, however, I knew that a letter to Clara must follow. She would know that Kate had heard from me and she did not deserve the pain of thinking that I refused even to write to her. Torn between honesty and the reality of our situation, I finally wrote:

My Dear Clara,

You are *"my dear Clara" and always will be. It is not lack of love that keeps me from you, I promise. But Clara—I can't. I owe my parents too much; they stood by me when I might have lost everything—how can I let them down so severely for a second time? I wish—no, I don't wish that it were different, for how could I wish my parents less loving? I wish it did not hurt you too, my love.*

Please write to me. I need the succour of some contact with you, though I know I ought not to ask it of you. I'm glad that you have Kate and Feverley to bear you company.

Love always,

Serena.

When I sealed the letter, I knew that Clara would be able to see that it had been cried over; the lines were sometimes smudged and blurred by tears. I was torn between shame at my weakness and an even greater guilt borne of the knowledge that part of me wished her to know that I had cried, that I truly cared, though my actions might suggest otherwise. I kissed the letter before letting it go, but that she would never know.

CHAPTER EIGHTEEN

June

It was tranquil at home, but I was not happy and my parents knew it. I tried my best to interest myself in local goings-on. The Freemans and the Lances were back to their usual rivalries, but what had passed between them over Germaine's death suggested to me that they enjoyed the drama of the dispute rather than caring deeply for subject of the dispute itself. My father's brood mare birthed a male foal. One of our servants asked permission to marry another. These were all the small, everyday parts of life in the country.

Behind it all, though, was Clara. I could not forget. I missed Kate, too, and Feverley. Kate's bracing conversation and light-hearted take on life would have been very useful to allay my unhappiness, my loneliness. We socialised with few people in the close district, and I had become accustomed to being surrounded by friends. My mother, bless her, did her best. Not, as when I had returned in disgrace, by finding me work, but by encouraging me in all the things she knew I loved to do. I believe I must have improved my piano playing more in those months at home than in all the years previously, though I shied away from love songs and the like. My father, too, though he said little, looked at me with such care in his eyes I knew that I could have done nothing else but return home. How could I hurt these wonderful people who loved me so much?

One June morning I made my weekly sojourn into the village. The trip had become a welcome habit, and afforded me at least a bit of casual conversation with the shopkeepers and an occasional neighbour. I made stops at the apothecary, tailor and milliner before heading home, bearing parcels and gossip alike.

I knew something had happened the moment I saw Mama's face. I burst in, full of news about the most recent truce between the Lances and Freemans, but my words faltered as I noticed my mother's expression.

"Mama, what's wrong?"

She shook her head in a pitiful effort to deny my query. "Wrong? Why should anything be wrong?" But she did not deny that something had happened. I knew my mother too well to be misled by her prevarication.

"Have I…" I almost drew back from the question, fearing the answer. "…done something to displease you?"

"No." Her face softened. "No, my Serena."

She held open her arms and I ran into them, and buried my head on her shoulder. I still had no inkling of what had happened; I only knew my mother wanted—needed—my support.

"Father…has something happened to Father?"

Her arms tightened around me, and for an awful second I believed I had stumbled upon the truth. "No, my darling. Everyone is well. All is well." Mama hesitated. "In your absence today, we…had a visitor."

"Mm-hm?" Mentally I called down coals of fire on the visitor who had distressed Mama so deeply.

Mama unclasped my hands from her neck, and led me to the chaise longue. She slipped a hand into my own, the other picking at a nonexistent loose thread in her skirt.

"Lady Routledge—Clara—came to visit your father and me."

I stood up unconsciously, but the pull of my mother's fingers on mine made me resume my seat.

"Clara?"

"Oh my darling," Mama said, and her voice was low. "How could you let us think what we did?"

I could not pretend to misunderstand her. "It was true, in the main." My eyes, despite myself, *would* fill with tears. "All that Lady Maria told you was true."

"All save one—the most important point."

I looked at her, and a tear forced its way down my cheek. "What difference would it have made?" I asked her. "You were right. I am…unnatural. What difference would it have made to tell you I was not alone? A sin"—and I choked a little—"is no less a sin if one does not sin alone."

"Serena." My mother stroked my hair, as if I were a small girl once more. I leaned my head against hers, needing the comfort only a parent could give. "You know the difference," she said gently. "You knew we would believe—would have to believe, no matter how unlikely—that you assaulted your dearest friend in her own house. Lady Maria spoke with such authority. Why did you offer no denial?"

I pressed closer to her. The words came haltingly, for I did not like admitting how hurt, how painfully, soul-deep hurt I had been at the time. "I thought I'd lost…everything," I whispered. "Everything. I thought I had nothing more to lose, yet Clara had. But there was one more thing to lose, too. Your trust in me."

Mama put her arms around me and held me tightly. I could feel the dampness of her tears on my head. "Oh Serena, my dear daughter. You let your father and I think *that* of you, so Clara would not suffer? And we—I—"

"You comforted me." My own tears wet her neck. "You did not reject me."

"I should have trusted you!" My mother's voice was anguished. "And you, all alone, bearing that on top of…"

"You…you didn't turn me out." I bit my lips and remembered the journey homewards, and how I had wondered whether my parents would disown me on the spot. "I feared you might." I took a breath. "And Mama, it *was* true. I had done…what she said. Clara and I…"

It was Mama's turn to cut me off. "Yes, darling. Clara *and* you. I would have been—indeed, I confess I am—disappointed, even shocked by such behaviour, for it is not in the natural way of things, darling; you know that as well as I. But we would have tried to understand—no, we *would* have understood—that it was borne of love between you both. What distressed us the most—in particular your father, for Matthew Battersley has always been so great a friend of his—was the thought that you had assaulted Clara in her own home, against her will."

"You won't tell Father?" I asked. I lifted my head and wiped a hand across my eyes, now blurry from crying.

"Dear, I must." Mama, too, brushed at my lashes to dry my tears. Her own face was equally stained, but her thought, as always, was only for me. "You know I must."

"It's over." I swallowed hard, trying to stanch any lingering sobs. "What use is there in bringing it up again? It changes nothing. I don't want him to feel bitterly toward Clara, toward her father. Even if he never mentions it to Mr. Battersley, the betrayal will be there, in the air, between them."

"And if I do not tell him," Mama responded, "it will be between you and your father forever." She hushed my protest with an upraised palm. "I know. You will say that nothing will have changed. Therefore, Serena, I shall give you the one argument to which I know you cannot object. If I do not tell your father what Clara has told me, the shadow will lie between him and me; a secret between us. Would you ask that of me?"

She was right; I could not protest that line of reasoning, particularly after all I had put my parents through. "No."

Mama reached into her reticule and took out a handkerchief to wipe her eyes. We sat in silence for a minute or two, and recovered our composure.

"Serena, why did you return home when you did last month?"

I had anticipated the question, but had hoped that she would not ask it. Still, I owed my mother the truth. "Must I say?" I pleaded.

She gazed at me thoughtfully. "It seemed…" She stopped, as she searched for the right words. "During her visit today, it seemed as though Clara cared for you still. And you? Do you still care?"

I could not look at her. "I do not want to disappoint you again."

"Tell me, dearest," my mother encouraged. "Don't you know you could never disappoint me? I only wish to know what is truly in your heart."

I steeled myself then, and raised my eyes to Mama's. "I have never stopped caring for Clara."

It was true, everything Kate had said to me was true. Only someone you loved could cause you so much pain. Kate's engagement to Feverley had been a shock, but accepting my parting from her had not caused me anything like the heartache I had felt over Clara. I loved Kate dearly, as a friend, but Clara… was so much more than that.

My mother nodded thoughtfully. "And Clara? Surely her marriage…?" Mama came to a halt, but I knew too well what she was thinking: surely once Clara had been married and experienced relations as they should be, she would not wish for a return to the abnormal practises of her youth?

"I think…" I began falteringly. I started again. "I know she still cares," I said quietly.

"So you came home." My mother's tone was wondering. She caught up my hand and held it tight. "You did the right thing, Serena," she said.

Then why, I thought, though I did not ask, *does it hurt so much*?

* * *

I missed Clara. That was undoubted truth. Even during my months in London, when I had had Kate and Feverley and an entire host of decadent pursuits, I had missed her. Now, at home, in the very house where I had so often played with my dearest love, or out in a village where her face and name were as well known as my own, the ache increased tenfold.

Clara had proved herself truer than I had previously imagined. She had not, as I had thought, allowed her mother to place all the blame for our love on me. Knowing nothing of Lady Maria's written accusations, Clara had lived with her mother's criticisms of her behaviour, day after day, hour after hour. If she had taken the first opportunity out of that situation, I could not blame her. It was understandable after all, especially since she had accepted Lord Routledge under the threat of her own and my exposure.

After visiting my parents, Clara made no attempt to contact me. I knew that she had left it to me to make the next move. She had demonstrated her willingness to defy the world for my sake, not only going against her mother's explicit demands by her association with me but also by telling my parents all that had happened, risking exposure after admitting her collusion in our affair. Perhaps she was a pragmatist, working on the theory that my parents—as well has hers—had too much to lose by admitting that their daughter was guilty of perversion.

But that did not fit with the Clara I knew and loved. I, perhaps, might have stepped down that road. Kate, certainly, would have acted with a definite knowledge of calculated risk, but Clara had ever been one to act first and fear the consequences only later. Or perhaps that is unfair. Clara knew, when she visited Father and Mama, that there was a danger in what she had to say, but being my honest, direct Clara she saw the danger to herself without considering that the very nature of her confession must make my parents unwilling to reveal it. As I told Mama when she confronted me, Clara's complicity made my own behaviour no more pardonable. In the eyes of my parents, yes, I understood the difference. The world, however, would not see the rightness of her truth-telling, it would see only the sin we had both committed. Verbal declarations of love might be acceptable (or even *a la mode*) between women. Physical demonstrations such as she and I had shared were beyond forgiveness.

I knew the moment Mama told Father of Clara's visit, although he spoke not a word about it. I think Mama had warned him not to raise the subject. But in his eyes, I saw a warmth, a relief, nonetheless. As with Mama, his mien was tinged with pain. I think he, too, condemned himself for having believed the worst of his only daughter. I truly felt for them both, for with my admission of fault, I had given them little choice. At the same time, the revelation made me feel as if I had shed thirty pounds in weight. I don't think I had really realised quite how much their belief that I could possibly assault a friend had hurt me. None of us spoke of it, but we all knew.

But then, Clara. Clara. My wonderful, true Clara. I sent her a note three days after her visit. It bore two words: "thank you." Only two words, but they sufficed. She had given up—had chosen to give up—everything for me, if I would but agree. And I knew more and more certainly that I could do nothing else.

That night, after a quiet dinner, I faced my parents with both resolve and trepidation. From the moment I began to speak, their faces turned sombre.

"I've something I must tell you," I said. "Forgive me if I speak too candidly."

Father had reached out to take Mama's hand in his. For a man as undemonstrative as he, it was an unusual gesture. "The time for reticence has passed, has it not, my daughter?" he said quietly.

"I think we know what it is you wish to say, Serena." Mama moved a little closer to Father, as if she needed to feel his physical support. "You intend to return to London, do you not?"

I nodded. "I must. I have tried so hard to forget, to be happy here. But I miss Clara too much. I need to be with her. I'm sorry."

"We know that you are unhappy," my father said. "We have perhaps borne inadequate witness to your suffering."

"No!" I half-reached out a hand to them both, and then dropped it to my side. "You have been so kind, so loving toward me. You are the best parents any girl could have, but I fear I am not the best daughter."

"Oh, Serena," Mama sighed softly. "That is not true."

"Our relationship has been marred by too many misunderstandings over the past few years," I continued, trying to keep my voice steady. "The very least I owe you now is the truth. I thought I would have to learn to live without Clara, but the truth is the only thing lying between us now is my fear of your disapproval. I don't want to hurt you, but I can't bear living this lie. I love Clara, and she loves me, and we want to be together."

"I cannot say that your wish comes as a great surprise to us," Father said heavily. "Since her visit, your mother and I have suspected as much."

"I'm sorry," I repeated. "I know I have disappointed you."

"Serena," my mother said, "you cannot expect us to be pleased by this…this…turn of events." (I knew the word "perversion" trembled on the tip of her tongue. I was grateful that she cared enough, even now, to bite it back.)

"I know my decision is difficult for you to understand." Determined as I was not to cry, I felt tears pricking at the backs of my eyes. My father's face was grim, and I felt horribly sure he would not be able to forgive me. "Father…" I started, but he interrupted me.

"Whatever you do, whatever you *are*, Serena"—and his face creased with unhappiness—there is one thing that will never change. You are still our daughter." He paused, and released Mama's hand, as he leaned back in his chair and looked steadily at me. "You love Clara?"

"Yes, Father." My voice was resolute. "More than anything."

"And your mother and I love you, more than anything," he said. "Then you must go, and we must prove our love by allowing you to go."

Tears cascaded down my cheeks. My mother reached out her hand to me, and I held it as tightly as I could, and raised our conjoined hands to my lips. Father stood and placed a hand on my shoulder, and I was humbled by their warmth and generosity, even when they did not—could not—understand. I thought of Clara's child, little Rosalind, and hoped Clara and I could give her the same sort of love my parents had for me: a love which was never withheld, a love which sought a child's happiness even over one's own.

"Thank you," I whispered, my head bowed. "I know I do not deserve your love, but I will try to be worthy of it. I promise I will not shame you. Clara's and my relationship…" Despite my tears, my heart could not help but leap at the words I spoke, at the knowledge that Clara and I would soon be reunited, this time forever. "…must, I know, always be a secret from the world. But your love, oh, Mama, Father, you cannot know how much your love means to me."

"We love you, dear," Mama said quietly. "Be happy."

CHAPTER NINETEEN

July

That night I wrote to Clara, asking her permission to come and stay—I did not say for how long—and it was a long few days before her reply returned, days in which I became unreasonably convinced that she had changed her mind and would turn me down. But, just as I had sent her a two-word note earlier, I received one from Clara this time. It said, simply, *Please come.* A row of kisses had been pressed underneath, nothing more.

My parents would have had me stay longer, but I stuck firmly to my resolve, and they saw me off with love and best wishes on Saturday afternoon. I had sent no further response to Clara, intending to make my arrival my answer.

At a quarter past seven o'clock at night, weary and travel-stained, I reached Clara's doorstep, my clothes in a bandbox at my feet.

"I'm here…I'm here to see Lady Routledge," I stammered.

Clara's butler gave me a look of distinct disapproval. The hour was not appropriate, in his correct world, for a social call. It was, however, not his place to suggest that his employer was out.

"Is Lady Routledge expecting you?" he asked.

"Yes," I assured him. "She is."

His eyes glanced briefly down at the large bandbox. I could not really blame him for his silent disapprobation. In polite circles it was, to say the least, unusual for any guest to arrive with suitcase in hand and a demand to see the lady of the house.

"Your name, madam?" He had met me before. At a different hour, he would have taken pride in knowing precisely who I was. His query was offered merely to make me feel awkward.

"Miss Coleridge."

"Very well." He suddenly stiffened into the perfect servant. "Pray wait whilst I inquire whether Lady Routledge is in."

I inclined my head as regally as I knew how, and waited. I was not kept long. Clara, careless of appropriate etiquette, almost flung herself down the stairs.

"Serena," she said, her eyes shining.

I immediately forgave the punctilious butler for his original coldness. It was clear he adored Clara; his entire expression had changed from forbidding to one of almost fatherly benevolence at the sight of her happiness.

"Clara." I took her hands in mine and lifted them to my mouth.

"Have you come…?" Her voice faltered with hope and anxiety.

"To stay." My eyes met hers. "To be your companion. If you'll have me."

"If!" Clara recollected herself. "Barnes, get someone to take Miss Coleridge's luggage to her room. The blue room, next to mine. And tell the chef to set dinner back. There are," she added, as she leaned close to my ear, "more important appetites to assuage than hunger. Come, Serena." She took me into her room, and closed the door.

"Oh, Clara."

We were in each other's arms. There was a sense of *rightness* about being together, body against soft female body. Her mouth sought and found mine, and we were kissing. She clasped a hand behind my head to pull me closer, to deepen the kiss until I thought I might die from the heat flooding through my body. I pulled her to the bed and we lay together. Her hands roved all over me, whilst I kissed her face over and again—eyebrow, cheek, forehead, nose—anywhere and everywhere I could.

"Let me remember you," she whispered, gentling her hands across my curves. She ran her fingers teasingly down the bodice of my dress.

"And you?" I asked.

She flushed a little. "I am different now."

"I love you no less," I assured her, stripping her of her dress and chemise. "Your breasts are firmer, heavier"—I kissed them—"and your body rounder. And, and…oh Clara, I love you more," I whispered, and knelt down to press kisses against that special, secret place from which little Rosalind had been birthed.

She was beautiful, beautiful. The taste of her so familiar, so loved. She murmured noises of encouragement as I pleasured her. Her hands entangled in my hair, her breathing quickened. I remembered all these delights so well, and yet they were better than any of my memories. She gasped as a wave of pleasure washed through her, and I looked up to see tears in her eyes, tears which were matched in my own.

"And you, Serena," she whispered. "May I not touch you?" I smiled, and unbuttoned my dress with faintly trembling fingers. Clara saw the tremble, and put her own hands (warm, loving) over mine. "That is my responsibility," she said.

She was slow and gentle and delighted me with all the smaller caresses I had not taken the time to do for her. She kissed each area of skin revealed, and my body was suffused with warmth. Finally, we were naked together, flesh against flesh, holding each other as if we would never let go. Clara's hand slipped between my legs. Her fingers rubbed my sensitive nub until my sight went fuzzy and I could think of nothing, only feel. I buried my head on her shoulder as my body convulsed, my tremors ran through her as if we were one entity, not two.

We lay together a long time after that, in each other's arms—where we belonged. Nothing much was said. It had all been said before. We were together, we were in love. Nothing else mattered.

"You will stay?" Clara asked me, several times, as if she feared my answer would change.

"As long as you will have me."

"Then, until forever," she murmured, and kissed my mouth and neck.

"Yes." Forever. It had a good sound. Together we would live and love, raise little Rosalind, continue our friendship with Feverley and Kate, and dance with many a man at many a ball. Then, we would come home to fall into each other's arms once more. Forever.

I am blessed.

Bella Books, Inc.
Women. Books. Even Better Together.
P.O. Box 10543
Tallahassee, FL 32302
Phone: 800-729-4992
www.bellabooks.com